TOM GATES

BISCUITS

So many!

BANDS

(AND VERY) BIG

PLANS

By Liz Pichon

(Who's not in a band - yet.)

Only draw in the book if it's YouRS OK?

Scholastic Children's Books
An imprint of Scholastic Ltd

Euston House,
24 Eversholt Street, London, NW1 1DB, UK
Registered office: Westfield Road, Southam,
Warwickshire, CV47 0RA
SCHOLASTIC and associated logos are trademarks and/or
registered trademarks of Scholastic Inc.
First published in the UK by Scholastic Ltd, 2018
Copyright © Liz Pichon Ltd, 2018

The right of Liz Pichon to be identified as the author and illustrator of
this work has been asserted by her.
ISBN 978 1407 19146 1
A CIP catalogue record for this book is available from the British Library.
All rights reserved.

Printed by CPI Group (UK) Ltd, Croydon, CR0 4YY
Papers used by Scholastic Children's Books are made
from wood grown in sustainable forests.

13 5 7 9 10 8 6 4 2

(This one))

HOORAY

← THIS IS **THE**

BOOK

I've BEEN WAITING FOR

BECAUSE

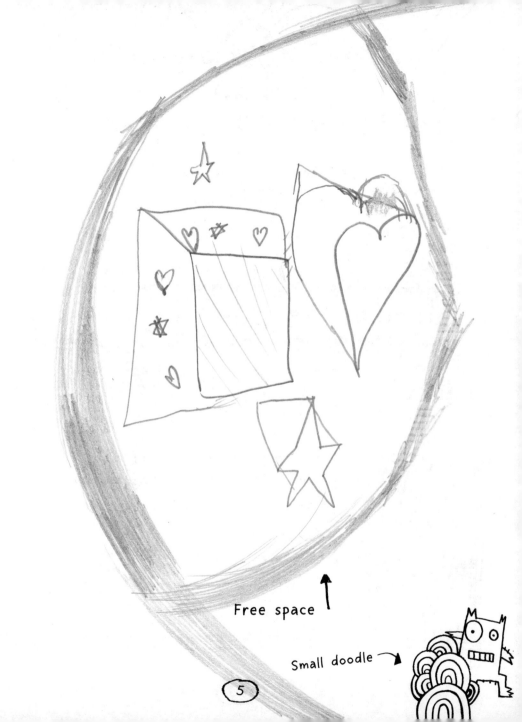

Free space

Small doodle

Y ou can use this BOOK to AVOID doing

boring stuff like chores or

cutting your toenails. Who likes doing that?
No one that I know.
(Unless Marcus Meldrew does. I'll have to ask him.)

I do...

H ere are **my** TOP TIPS for you:

1. Just HOLDING this book can make you look BUSY.

Tom, can you take these towels upstairs?

I need to put my BOOK down FIRST...

Oh, don't worry, I'll do it.

2. Parents and teachers are less likely to bother you if you are reading. (FACT.)

3. Try pretending your BOOK is part of your homework, even if it's not.

4. **ALWAYS** have your book with you so you can **READ** at any time.

(Just keep reading, just keep reading.)

I hope these tips will be useful for you. (They will be.)
Enjoy reading and doodling just like I do.

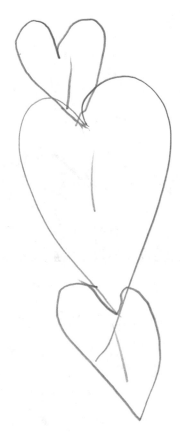

EVIDENCE →

Derek and Norman are coming over to my house later to write some NEW songs.

It's very important that we don't get distracted by anybody or ANYTHING ...

unless it's a snack break. THAT's allowed.

Woo-hoo! Hooray! YES!

Snacks

We decided to get together for an emergency **DOGZOMBIES** band practice after what happened in school yesterday.

(This is what happened.)

It was break time, and a group of us were chatting about our favourite BANDS. (As you do.)

We all agreed that **DUDE3** were the BEST BAND EVER. Apart from Marcus, who said,

DUDE3 aren't THAT good.

But he was just being awkward (nothing new there). I know he likes them really, because I've seen him at a **DUDE3** concert jumping around and **CHEERING**. So I ignored him and said THIS instead:

YEAH!

"How about **DOGZOMBIES**?
We're a GOOD BAND, aren't we?"

I was sort of making a joke, but when nobody answered I thought they hadn't heard me. So I said it again, only **much** **louder** this time.

"I MEAN, EVERYONE LIKES **DOGZOMBIES**, RIGHT?"

Derek and Norman put up their hands.

WE DO!

"Of course you both LIKE them – you're in the band," I pointed out.

"You're OK — not the best band, though. There's loads of bands better than you," Indrani told us, which was a bit HARSH.

"I can't say you're my FAVOURITE band as I haven't heard you play for AGES," AMY said, which was true, I suppose.

"I'VE heard you play and you're definitely NOT MY favourite band," Marcus added.

It just would have been nice if SOMEONE could have said we were a good band.

Then Norman jumped up and started shouting. "You lot haven't heard ALL the NEW songs we're writing.

DOGZOMBIES are going to be EVEN BETTER than DUDE3."

"IT'S **TRUE,**" Derek agreed.

"WE SO ARE!" I added, doing air punches,
while all the time thinking,

WHAT new songs?

Don't tell me – your NEW songs are
all about caramel wafers!

Marcus said, like that was a **BAD** idea.
(It was actually a very GOOD idea.)

"Maybe. Maybe not," I told him, being mysterious.

Then Derek kept it all going by saying,

"We've been very busy, and our songs are

TOP SECRET. So you'll just have to wait to

hear them. But there is ONE thing I can say..."

"What's THAT?" Marcus wanted to know.
"THEY ARE AWESOME SONGS!"
Derek was managing to make the whole NEW SONG
thing sound very exciting. Even I was impressed.
It made me really want to get writing, that's for sure.

Then Marcus told me,

"If you **DO** write about caramel wafers, remember it was **MY idea**, OK?"

"Hmmmmm," I said as Florence began waving her hands in the air to get our attention.

"Ooh, ooh, I forgot – my favourite band is

One Dimension!

They're AM-MAZ-ZING!"

"Yeah! I really like them too," Solid told us, which was a surprise.

"Their NEW song is SO good, isn't it?" Indrani added.

Then EVERYONE started to talk about **One Dimension** and they all agreed with Florence about what a GREAT BAND they are.

So good!

Love them.

 "I know **ALL** the words to their songs," **AMY** said.

 "Me too." Indrani smiled and started to **SING.** Let's ALL sing! ♪♪

It wasn't long before a **WHOLE** group of kids had gathered round to join in as well.

LET'S ALL SING TOGETHER!

Even Brad Galloway stopped for the singalong like he couldn't help himself.

I didn't want to be left out, but not knowing the words made it harder to sing along.

La la...   La. la.
Mmmm...   Mmm.
La. la.   AGH...

Florence kept **GLARING** at me in a "you're spoiling the moment, please stop" kind of way.

"We'll HAVE to write new songs now, won't we?" I whispered to Derek and he agreed.

"Let's meet up at the weekend. I've got some ideas."

It was a **GOOD PLAN**, and once Norman stopped singing I'd tell him about it.

LET'S ALL SING TOGETHER! LET'S ALL SING...

Who knew Norman was SUCH a BIG FAN of **One Dimension?** He'd kept that quiet.

Whatever the weather

LET'S ALL SING TOGETHER! LET'S ALL SING ...

For the rest of the day, I couldn't get the tune of "**LET'S ALL SING**" out of my head.

LET'S ALL SING Even when I was trying to do work, THAT chorus kept popping up at all the wrong times.

LET'S ALL SING....

TOM, LOOK OUT!

LET'S ALL SING!

When Mr Fullerman said,

"Tom – what's the answer to the question?" I blurted out...

"LET'S ALL SING!..."

– **NO,** let's **NOT.** Sorry, sir, I don't know."

It was <u>embarrassing</u>. **DOGZOMBIES** really need some **NEW** catchy songs that stick in your

head like that one.

Groan...

I wake up SUPER EARLY, although I can't actually open my eyes. ➡ I try my best, but it's not happening. It's a **HUGE** struggle, so I don't bother for a while. I can't stay in bed too long because the rest of the band are coming over to my house later and we have a LOT of things to do.

OK, I'm getting UP...

... here I go ...

... in a minute.

I am ... really going ... to

... get ... up soon.

I'm surprisingly **tired** this morning, and I THINK it has something to do with all the remembering I did yesterday, and it wasn't even for HOMEWORK.

When I came back from school, I decided to copy out ALL the WORDS from **One Dimension's "LET'S ALL SING"** so I could learn them off by heart.

Writing them in my notebook seemed like a good idea, until I realized where my notebook WAS. I'd only gone and left it in Delia's room! I was looking at some **ROCK WEEKLYS** when she came back and nearly caught me... I had to make a *RUN* for it

Uh-oh... *FAST.*

THUMP
THUMP
THUMP

SNEAKING back in to find my notebook was tricky, but I managed to get it and a few more copies of **ROCK WEEKLY** as well.

Once I had it, I started to write out the lyrics and add my own doodles, which made them look way more interesting (I think). And it helped me to remember the words off by heart, so NOW if anyone breaks into SONG, I'll be able to join in and Florence can give her **BAD stares** to someone else.

MY NOTEBOOK ⟩ → → - → →.

LET'S ALL SING TOGETHER!

(FOR NOW)

By **One Dimension**

Pictures by me – Tom Gates

The band

Doodle legend

Open your EYES

It's a sunny day

The SKY is BLUE

We'll be there for you

(FOR NOW)

Come on let's **SING** together

While we have a **V**oice

We can sing for ever

Ooh ooh ooh

We all **SING** together

WHOA WHOA WHOA

Try and make things better

Ooh ooh ooh

Let's
SING

This SPACE is for you to write your own song or poem – or doodle!

x2

x2 Hey little butterysly

Spead yare Wengs
and Slee and
When I Come
home and
I Spreed
Me Wings I Slee
a little bit mar
high

THE

End

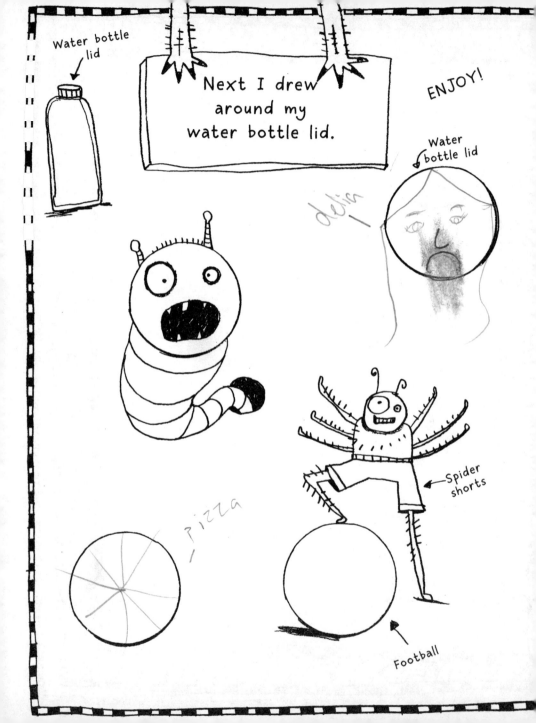

Water bottle lid

Next I drew around my water bottle lid.

ENJOY!

Water bottle lid

delia

pizza

Spider shorts

Football

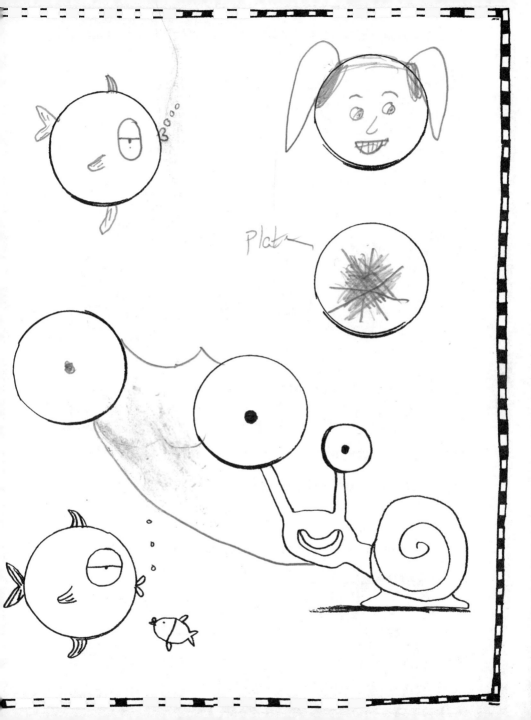

Plat

(No wonder I'm still tired. I did a LOT of drawing.)

When 😣 Marcus said we should write a song

about [caramel] [wafers], I thought

it was a pretty good idea. The trouble is if

we ACTUALLY write one, he'll go ON and ON

about how it was ALL his idea FOR EVER.

I can see it now...

> That song was ALL **my** idea!

Old Marcus

But since I spent SO LONG in bed, I used the

time WELL and thought of something ELSE

we could write about instead. I don't know WHY

we haven't done this before.

We need to write a song about ...

> BISCUITS.

Awake now!

We can sing about LOADS of different types of biscuits, not just wafers – for those people who don't like wafers.
(IF those people actually exist.)

Yum

WAFER

DOGZOMBIES AND BISCUITS

What's not to like?

We'll call it

Biscuit tin

which already sounds like a **HIT** to me

Yes!

and we haven't even started writing it yet.

The thought of biscuits has encouraged me to LEAP out of bed, get dressed and then make a ➜ **BISCUIT LIST**.

SO, in no particular order:

Biscuit List :)

  **WAFER**

(all kinds, but caramel

are the best)

 Chocolate Chip

Chocolate Digestives

 (side view)   Custard
Creams

Iced Biscuits

 (with sprinkles)

Lack of
chocolate
→

  Oat Biscuits

(preferably with chocolate)

 Shortbread (in any shape)

This is a good way to start my day.
I carry on with a doodle...

 I stop drawing because I'm getting hungry. Before I head downstairs, I check under my bed to make sure the **ROCK WEEKLYS** I borrowed from Delia's room are still there.

They are.

I pick up one and start *flicking* through it when I spot a WHOLE section on

OLD BANDS.

I recognize some of them from Derek's dad's record collection. They wore VERY BIG FLARED TROUSERS and HUGE platform shoes in those days.

Vinyl records

Whoa!

How did they get on stage?
Dad had a pair like that once, but I
don't think he was ever in a band...
(Or WAS he? I might have to ask him again.)
Looking at the photographs of the **OLD** bands,
I think they used to dress up a lot more in the past.

These **ROCK WEEKLYS** have

lots of interesting

things in them.

(Dad in a band...)

Mmmmmmm....

Funny!

LOOK at THAT!

ROCK WEEKLY

Nice guitar.

I've been thinking that **DOGZOMBIES** could try out a NEW look to go with the songs (that we haven't written yet).

Maybe not as **WILD** as the bands in **ROCK WEEKLY**, but a new T-shirt design might work? I'll show these pictures to Derek and Norman when they get here. So to make sure I don't forget which magazines the pictures are in, I mark each page with a sock (obviously).

I know they'll find the photos **FUNNY**.

There's a whole section on **DUDE 3** that I haven't seen before too, which takes up THREE (almost clean) socks.

I've noticed lots of bands wear sunglasses all the time, like Delia does. Only, the bands look cool.

Delia just looks *fed up* or slightly

FURIOUS

or **BOTH**.

Not all bands look cool, though...

(It's the hair!)

70ˢ 80ˢ 90ˢ ROCK BANDS

OLD bANDS WITH STYLE

His hair looks like Rooster!

Ha! Ha!

I'm trying to imagine what DOGZOMBIES would look like with THAT band style. Probably something like THIS.

I draw Rooster with some OLD BAND STYLE.

Like Granddad's wig! →

44

Dog suit

HA!
HA! HA!

45

I can't stop laughing
at my drawings of Rooster...

HA! HA!
HA! HA! HA! Ha!
HA! HA!
ha! ha! HA! ha!
HA! HA!
HA! ha! ha! ha!

I'm still LAUGHING when Delia interrupts me by BAnGinG on the door.

BASH
BASH
BASH!

"TOM! HAVE YoU BEEN IN my ROOM AgAIN?"

"WHAT? NO!
Don't come in!"

I shout, jumping up and trying to hide all the

ROCK WEEKLYS at the same time as holding

the door SHUT. I accidentally knock over some

water with GREEN

paint in it that

SPILLS over the

magazines and drips on

to the floor.

"DON'T GO in my room!" Delia shouts.

"Don't YOU come in MY room

EVER!" I say back to her.

"You'll have to come out here sometime," Delia says.

"I'm staying HERE," I tell her.

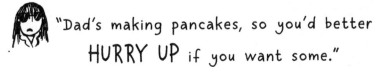
"Dad's making pancakes, so you'd better
HURRY UP if you want some."

"Oh..."

(49)

This could be a TRICK to make me LEAVE my room so she can have a SNOOP and see if I've taken her magazines.

I am WISE to this, but I also don't want to RISK missing out on pancakes.

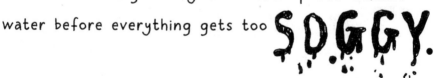

"You can GO away now," I tell her, then I listen to make sure she's gone downstairs. Once it's safe to move away from the door, I GRAB

the nearest thing to try and WIPE up the GREEN water before everything gets too SOGGY.

"That's better," I say to myself, before I realize ...

ooo I've just used a pair of my pants to mop up with.

They're a bit GREEN now, so I STUFF them into a plastic cup, which gets them out of the way.

Mum gave me a whole stack of plastic cups after I ruined some fancy teacups with my paints. I could tell I was in trouble when she said,

TOM!
WHAT HAVE YOU DONE
TO THE CUPS?

Uh-oh... How was I supposed to know my paints wouldn't come off?

I thought the cups looked **much** nicer with all the EXTRA colours on them, but Mum didn't agree.

"If I ever get **FAMOUS,** these cups will be WAY MORE valuable with my PAINT decoration," I suggested.

"NICE TRY, TOM,

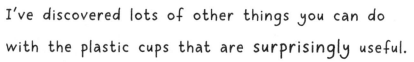

but from now on it's jam jars or PLASTIC CUPS only," Mum told me.

I've discovered lots of other things you can do with the plastic cups that are surprisingly useful.

Things you can make from plastic cups (or paper ones).

Telephone

Skittles

Small hat

My FAVOURITE thing to make with the CLEAR cups is a FACE changer.

This is how you make one. ⇨

1 Use a permanent black marker to draw a FACE on the cup.

2 Drop the cup into a second cup.

3 Draw on the second cup

over Delia's face.

4 TWIST the cups round to show the drawings.

I do a drawing of Delia on a NEW cup and ADD more extra silly things on another cup. I've already done a face changer for Mr Fullerman using the special

P E N Buster Jones gave me that draws on plastic (and other things Buster isn't supposed to draw on).

BUSTER WAS HERE

Then I take them down to breakfast so Delia can see my work. She's going to be VERY impressed. :)

(NOT...)

When I get to the kitchen, there are **NO** pancakes ANYWHERE because Delia was being **S**NAKEY and made all it up.

(Like I suspected!)

I'm glad I didn't *RUSH* downstairs and even MORE pleased that I made this **NEW** FACE CHANGER.

"Have you been in my room AGAIN?" Delia asks me.

"NO," I say quickly.

"Well you took your time coming down," she adds.

"I guessed there were **NO** pancakes, so why *HURRY?*"

"Actually, we DID have pancakes and they're **G**ONE. They were delicious too."

 **"YOU MISSED OUT, TOM."**

For a split second, I believe her.

"NO!"

I'm not very good at hiding my feelings about food.

Then Dad says, "Don't worry, she's kidding. I didn't make pancakes."

Which is a relief, although I would actually LIKE some pancakes.

I show Delia what I've been making to see her reaction.

"I made this face changer – recognize anyone?"

"Don't you have anything better to do?"

"Not really."

"**Come** on, you two, enough winding each other up. I wonder if it's going to rain today. Do either of you know?"

Dad is peering up at the sky, which does look a bit dark.

"It always rains," Delia says gloomily.

"I might need some more bin liners, then. They seem to be doing the trick on my leaky shed roof."

"Why do bin liners get used for everything in this family?"

For **ONCE** I find myself agreeing with Delia and thinking of the time Mum made me wear a bin liner

as a **COAT.**

"**W**hy don't you just get it fixed by someone who knows what they're doing?" she asks Dad.

"It's called using your initiative," he says while tapping his head with his finger.

Mum hears the end of their conversation and looks worried.

"**PLEASE** don't go climbing up on the shed roof if it's **dodgy,** Frank."

"I'm not going to do anything SILLY. The bin liners have worked perfectly well. I just need to add a few more to **REALLY** fix it!" Dad assures her, then he spots one of my FACE CHANGERS and picks it up.

"Did you make this?"

"**Ha!** LOOK, there's **Mr Fullerman** with lots of hair. I wouldn't take this to school, Tom. You don't want to get into trouble!" Dad LAUGHS, then he picks up Delia's Face changer. "Look at you, Delia! That's funny."

"So does Tom get into **Trouble** for drawing pictures of ME then?" she wants to know.

"The difference is, you do actually look like that," I tell her while holding my cup drawing next to her face. "SEE?" Delia tries to GRAB it from me, but I am WAY too fast.

"If you two BOTH stop annoying each other, I will make pancakes. Anything for a peaceful morning," Dad tells us.

60

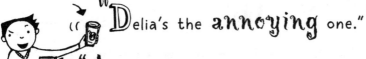

"Delia's the **annoying** one."

"**Annoying** is YOUR middle name."

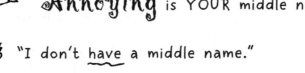

"I don't <u>have</u> a middle name."

"Do you two want pancakes or NOT?"
Dad asks us again.

"PANCAKES!" I shout.

Delia mumbles, "Thanks, Dad..."

CRACK

"Lovely family breakfast - so restful," Mum sighs.

While Dad's making pancakes, I add a few more
things to my FACE CHANGER.

 "You should make one of those with Uncle Kevin, Aunty Alice and the cousins. That would be FUNNY,"

Delia says as she watches me draw.

(Ha!)→

 "Ok, I will."

Then I TWIST the cups round and show Delia the EXTRA work I've been doing.

"HEY LOOK, you've got a beard now!"

 "Don't make me squash your plastic cup," she says.

An improvement, I think.

Here are some more
Delia doodles.

How to draw Delia –
with EXTRAS.

When Dad serves the pancakes, they're all in slightly **WEIRD** shapes.

"I'm feeling creative," he says. "It's a cat."

"Really? It doesn't look like a cat, and Delia's one doesn't look like a cat either," I point out.

"That's because it's a BIRD," Dad tells me.

"I'm not a little kid," Delia sighs.

"I'll have yours if you don't want it," I say helpfully with my **fork** POISED.

"No chance," Delia says and eats her bird pancake. They actually taste really nice, and while I'm scraping my plate, I remind everyone about my band practice later today.

Yum

 "Just so you know, me, Derek and Norman will be writing a lot of GREAT songs and we don't want to be disturbed."

I GLARE at Delia so she knows I mean HER. ⟹

 "Unless ... it's for snacks," I add quickly.

 "DON'T tell me I have to listen to you lot playing the SAME THING over and over again really badly," she grumbles.

 "You could always go OUT?" I suggest.

Mum steps in and says, "That's fine, Tom, but don't play TOO loudly and no full-on DRUMS. Well done for practising, though."

(Mum is more POSITIVE than Delia.)

Then she asks Dad a question.

"If you're FREE this morning, Frank, would you like to come with me to IK—"

{IKEA?} Before Mum can finish her sentence,

Dad interrupts her. "OH, what a shame! I'm

SO behind with my work, I can't go. And I need to

fix the shed roof too."

"If you're sure, I'll take Mavis instead

as she wanted to come."

"I'm SO sure. Bring back some tea lights."

Which means NOW I'll be relying on Dad

for any band snacks today.

I need to ask him a VERY important question.

"Dad, exactly how FULL is the

biscuit tin in your shed?"

"What biscuit tin?" he says.

"Your secret biscuit tin," I remind him.

"Even I know about it – we ALL do."

Delia joins in the conversation.

"We're writing a song about biscuits, so it's

research."

"We'll be needing quite a few to keep us going, I think." ☺

"I'll see what I can do – NOT that there's anything resembling a biscuit tin in my shed," he adds.

(Nice try, Dad.) ← Dad's not-so-secret biscuit tin

Mum pops her head back round the door to say, "Don't do anything DAFT, will you?"

"Listen to your mother..." Dad tells us.

"I was talking to YOU, Frank – be careful fixing the shed roof, OK?"

"I'll be fine!" Dad says confidently.

"**By** the time you come back we'll have written loads of good songs!" I tell Mum.

"I can't wait to hear them!" she says.

Hmmmm-

Delia adds, which is typical of her.

I go upstairs to make a VERY important SIGN.

I don't want Delia to *BARGE* into my room and SEE any of the ROCK WEEKLYS. Because THEN she'll know that I've been in her room.

Borrowed → magazines

I wasn't SN OO PING deliberately – I was only looking for magazines when I just happened to SPOT something else that was

VERY

INTERESTING.

DELIA'S DIARY

There was a big LOCK on the side, which made me want to read it even more. But I was very good and didn't, because I know it's private (and I couldn't get it open).

I'm hoping Delia won't notice it's been moved, because she would go CRAZY if she knew I'd even SEEN her DIARY. Then Mum and Dad would probably tell me off for going in her room as well. I could be in a lot of trouble. So that's another good reason to make a sign.

KEEP OUT

(Band practising)

There are LOTS of signs I could make, but this one's good for now.

Here are some other sign ideas.

IF YOU'RE CALLED
DELIA - BACK
AWAY NOW

Spare sign

Secret
bisness
go away
(only be shall enter
with thi snacks.

When **D**erek arrives, he likes my sign.

"But won't your sister just ignore it?"

"I'll make a **BARRIER** with pillows as well. That'll slow her down."

(It's a good plan.)

Derek checks out the other drawings I've done. "**Wow** - you've been busy. Nice use of socks, too."

He's found the **ROCK WEEKLYS,** so I point out the old band photos.

"**Check** out the bands' clothes! What do you think of them?"

Derek starts turning the pages REALLY slowly like he's studying them. Then he looks at one for a **LONG** TIME.

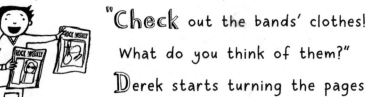

He's joking – so I have a GOOD LAUGH!

"THAT would be hilarious!"

I say, laughing some more.

 "No, seriously – I like this LOOK. I think it could work for us."

Huh? Derek doesn't sound like he's joking.

"We could start all over again. Reinvent ourselves. New songs and a completely NEW LOOK. Good idea, don't you think?"

"Hmmmmm. I'm not so sure. Couldn't we just get new T-shirts?" I say, trying to put Derek off the **WHOLE** NEW STYLE thing.

I don't think it's a G O O D idea at ALL.

"BUT WE'D LOOK AMAZING! The **BIG** hair is the BEST part!"

Now I'm SPEECHLESS and don't know what to say.

Derek is looking and waiting

for me to say something.

Normally we agree on most things.

I'm struggling to give him an answer.

I only showed him the pictures because I thought they were F U N N Y. Eventually, I say,

"I'm still not sure. Shall we ask Norman what he thinks?"

"OK – I bet he LOVES the idea," Derek says confidently.

(I hope not.)

I try and put it out of my mind while we're waiting for Norman to turn up. I show Derek my FACE CHANGER and we do some more drawings as well.

"How do you draw a **DOGZOMBIE**?"

Derek wants to know.

"That's easy, you can make ANYTHING into a **zombie** if you want. Just add...

scars, ╫╫╫ ╫╫

BIG STAREY EYES, ⊙⊙

dribble

and sharp TEETH. ⋎⋎⋎⋎

 "Good tip."

Here's how to draw **DOGZOMBIES** and other

zombie creatures...

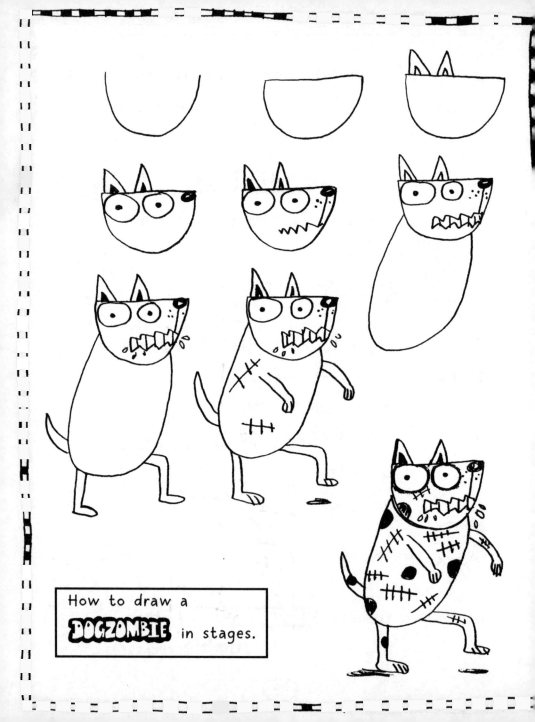

How to draw a
DOGZOMBIE in stages.

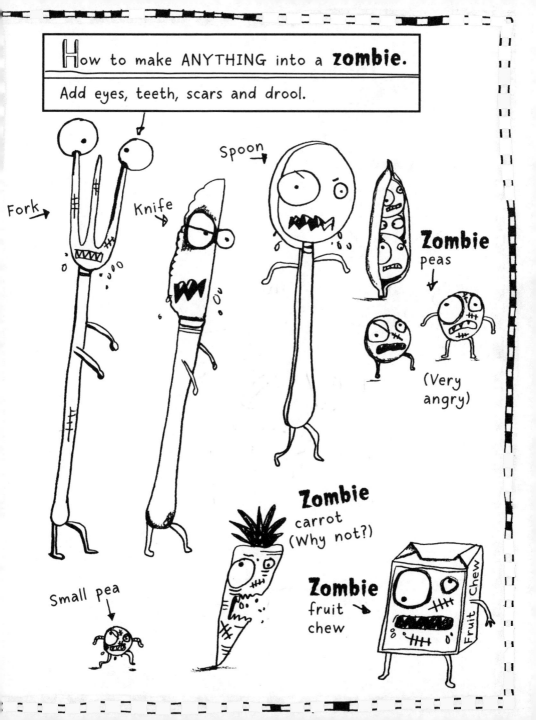

How to make ANYTHING into a **zombie.**

Add eyes, teeth, scars and drool.

Fork

Knife

Spoon

Zombie peas

(Very angry)

Small pea

Zombie carrot (Why not?)

Zombie fruit chew

Fruit Chew

Zombie fig roll

Grrrr...

looks adorable
but don't trast

Space for more **zombie** stuff

pencil

We've been drawing for a while when Derek says, "Now THIS would make an **AMAZING** band logo!" then shows me something that looks like a squiggle?

"Isn't that just a wiggly ～～ line?" I point out.

"**YES** — imagine THAT on a poster as <u>our</u> BAND LOGO. How brilliant would that be? (Derek is a bit too keen on this idea, which is a worry.)

"I kind of like our OLD dog logo better."
I decide to speak up this time.

"Come on, Tom. We need to be different, and THIS logo <u>IS</u> different. Don't be stuck in the past."

$\mathbb{D}$erek holds up the squiggle again very proudly.

He can see I don't like it.

Naaaaaah

"Let's ask $\mathbb{N}$orman when he gets here – we can take a VOTE then," $\mathbb{D}$erek tells me.

"Yes, let's," I say, because I'm **sure** $\mathbb{N}$orman will agree with me. This is NOT like $\mathbb{D}$erek at all, but I'm going along with him because once $\mathbb{N}$orman arrives he'll help sort things out and then we can get on with writing our songs.

But just in case, I draw a few more band logos myself. They still feature dogs (of course) and **zombies** (which makes sense).

$\mathbb{D}$erek decides to make his own FACE CHANGER. (I like it a lot more than his squiggle.)

Guess who?

Here are MY band logos.

Dog drool logo

Me as a

←**zombie**

As Derek and I don't seem to be agreeing on very much right now, I show him my biscuit list and tell him it's for a new song. We like the same biscuits, so this should be easier for sure.

 "That's GENIUS! Why haven't we done that before?"

"I KNOW!"

Which <u>reminds</u> me that Dad's supposed to be bringing up HIS biscuit tin.

I make another quick sign so he doesn't forget.

ALL
BISCUITS
WELCOME
(even plain ones)
DAD - don't forget!
☺

When the bell goes, we both rush downstairs to answer the door as we have a LOT of important decisions to make now.

DING

DING

DING

We open the door, and Norman is here ...

... but he's **NOT** on his own.

Alfie, his little brother, is with him. He's like a mini version of Norman, only a lot LiVELiER

(if that's even possible).

"Mum said I had to bring Alfie with me or I wouldn't be able to come over."

Hello, I'm Alfie.

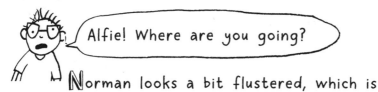

"I'm glad you're here, as we need to talk about some stuff..." I say to Norman as Alfie slips past and runs upstairs.

Alfie! Where are you going?

Norman looks a bit flustered, which is unusual for him. Then Alfie slides down the banister.

"WHEEEEEEEEEEEEE!"

"He'll be good later, I promise. I've brought things to keep him busy while we write songs."

Then Alfie runs upstairs again, but this time he doesn't come back down.

"Uh-oh – where's he gone?" Norman runs after him.

"This is going to be **FUN**," Derek whispers to me.

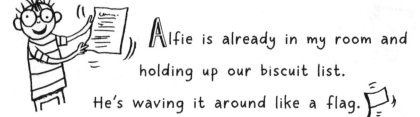

Alfie is already in my room and holding up our biscuit list.

He's waving it around like a flag.

"Alfie, please give that to me, it's important," I tell him, which makes him want to keep it even more. "It's for our song – we're making a LIST of biscuits."

"BISCUITS!

I want a biscuit!" Alfie repeats, then drops the list so he can have a look for biscuits. He starts by crawling under my bed.

"What's THIS?"

he says, pulling out the plastic cup with my GREEN pants inside.

"I can explain!" I say, but Alfie has already taken them out.

"NO!" I say as Alfie only

goes and puts my pants ...

...ON HIS HEAD.

"Alfie, they're Tom's PANTS, take them OFF your head!" Norman tells him in a slightly disgusted kind of way.

"EEEEEEEEwwwwww! They're GREEN!" Alfie says.

"There's a good reason for that!" I'm trying to explain, but Alfie drops them on the floor. "It's PAINT WATER!" I shout, but Alfie's asking about biscuits again.

Can I have a biscuit?

"Come on, Alfie, there's no biscuits here. Why don't you do some drawing instead?" Norman suggests. (It's SO funny listening to him being ALL SENSIBLE for a change.)

It seems to work, as Alfie sits down at my desk. OK. I give him some paper and pencils, and I'm about to MOVE the plastic cup of leftover paint water OUT of his way, when I get distracted by Derek, who's kicking my PANTS up in the air with his FOOT!

LOOK OUT!

Then Norman flicks them back at him and they FLY over Alfie's head, who ducks down and knocks over the last bit of paint water.

Whoops!

I manage to GRAB my pants in MID AIR (skills), then I use them to wipe up the splodges all over Delia's **ROCK WEEKLYS**. AGAIN. ☹

At least EVERYONE can see <u>NOW</u> why my pants are GREEN.  Then I stuff them in another plastic cup.

There, all done.

"Nobody needs to worry about my pants any more, OK?" I say.

Derek, Norman and Alfie all nod.

"Right – where were we?"

Derek picks up the ROCK WEEKLY with the old bands in it.

"That reminds me – Tom and I have been finding **NEW** styles for DOGZOMBIES. I think this look would be GREAT for us. What do you think, Norman?" Derek asks enthusiastically.

"Here's my idea for a NEW band logo too," he adds and holds up his squiggle.

I'm hoping Norman will agree with me, so I pull a few faces and say, "We'd LOOK SO SILLY like THAT, right? I'd rather have a new T-shirt instead!"

"Come on, Tom, we need a change!" Derek passes the magazines over to Norman ...

... who studies the pictures really carefully.

"What do you think, Norman?" I ask him.

"Hmmmmmmm..." he says.
(I'm pretty sure he's going to agree with me.)

Eventually, Norman says...

"I think it's a GREAT IDEA!"

WHAT?

YES!

Derek is happy.

"You're KIDDING! I can't believe you're both saying that!"

This could be our FIRST

REAL BAND FALLOUT

98

Derek and Norman carry on talking about how BRILLIANT it's going to be wearing NEW clothes and having such an AMAZING LOGO.

"I LOVE it. Don't you, Derek?"

"YES, Norman – it's going to be AMAZING!"

I can't BELIEVE what I'm hearing.

Even Alfie joins in.

I like the **squiggle!**

"What's wrong with our old BAND LOGO? DUDE3 wouldn't have a squiggle or wear those clothes!"

I'm pacing around my bedroom, so at first I don't notice what's going on.

Ha! Ha! Ha! Ha! Ha! Ha! Ha! Ha! Ha! Ha! Ha!

"YOUR FACE, TOM,
when I showed you that *squiggle!*"

 Derek and Norman are
laughing a LOT.

They were just pretending to like the new look.

NOW I GET IT!

I really **believed** you!

I can laugh now because I'm so relieved!

Alfie is laughing too, but he doesn't know why. "What's so FUNNY?" he asks us.

"This LOGO!" Derek says, which sets us all off again and we don't hear Dad knock on the door before he comes in.

"You lot seem to be enjoying yourselves. How's the songwriting going?" he asks us.

"Better now you've brought the biscuit tin!" I tell him.

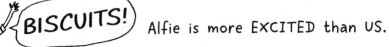

(BISCUITS!) Alfie is more EXCITED than US.

"I saw your sign, Tom. You can have <u>ONE</u> biscuit each from the top layer ONLY, OK?"

(It's better than nothing.)

Then Dad's phone goes off downstairs.

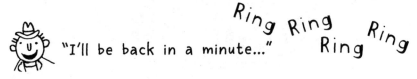

"I'll be back in a minute..."   Ring Ring Ring Ring Ring

I just need to get that. Help yourselves to one biscuit from the **TOP LAYER ONLY!"** Dad says, then rushes off.

We all study the biscuits and discover very quickly that there's a BIG problem. There are only **TWO** foil-covered biscuits on the top and we **ALL** want one of those.

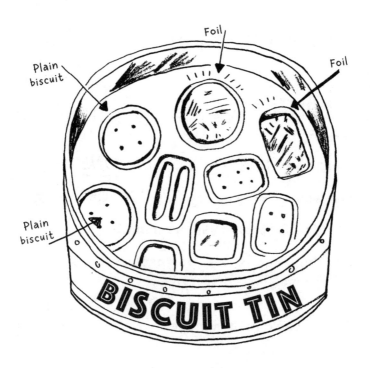

Foil

Plain biscuit

Foil

Plain biscuit

BISCUIT TIN

"Don't PANIC - I have a PLAN,"

I tell everyone.

To make it FAIR, I take the TWO foil biscuits from the **bottom** layer and SWAP them for two plain biscuits from the TOP.

That way we all get a foil-covered biscuit,

everybody's HAPPY - especially Alfie - and Dad won't see any **empty** spaces on the bottom layer. (Result!)

When Dad comes back, he's impressed we've not taken LOADS of biscuits.

"Well **done** for only taking ONE each, guys! I'll leave you to get on with your practice. How's The **BISCUIT** Song coming along?"

 MARSHMALLOWS! Alfie shouts.

"We're writing about biscuits, not marshmallows," I tell him.

"I'll look forward to hearing it!"

Dad smiles then lets us get on.

We have a look at our list as I pick up my guitar. Derek sets up his keyboard and Norman has his small drum. We're all ready to start when Alfie says, LOUDLY,

CAN I PLAY TOO?

and starts hitting Norman's drum ... A LOT.

"You're not in the band, Alfie. Can you do some drawing instead?"

Alfie! Stop!

"NO, I don't want to," Alfie says and keeps drumming. "I want to be in YOUR band."

(Uh-oh – this isn't going well.)

Alfie's not going to let us practise, I can tell.

We're going to need another

PLAN.

Then I remember an old shaker I made in school.
It's filled with rice and makes a nice noise.
Alfie can use THAT. It's not as annoying as the drum.
I go and get it for him.
"Hey, Alfie, look at this!"
He seems to like the shaker and
for a while it keeps him happy.
We get to carry on writing our biscuit
song and let Alfie do the SHAKING.
Everything is going well until Alfie ups his
shaking.

"SLOW down, Alfie! Less SHAKING!"
Norman tries to tell him, but he won't stop.
He's shaking SO MUCH ...

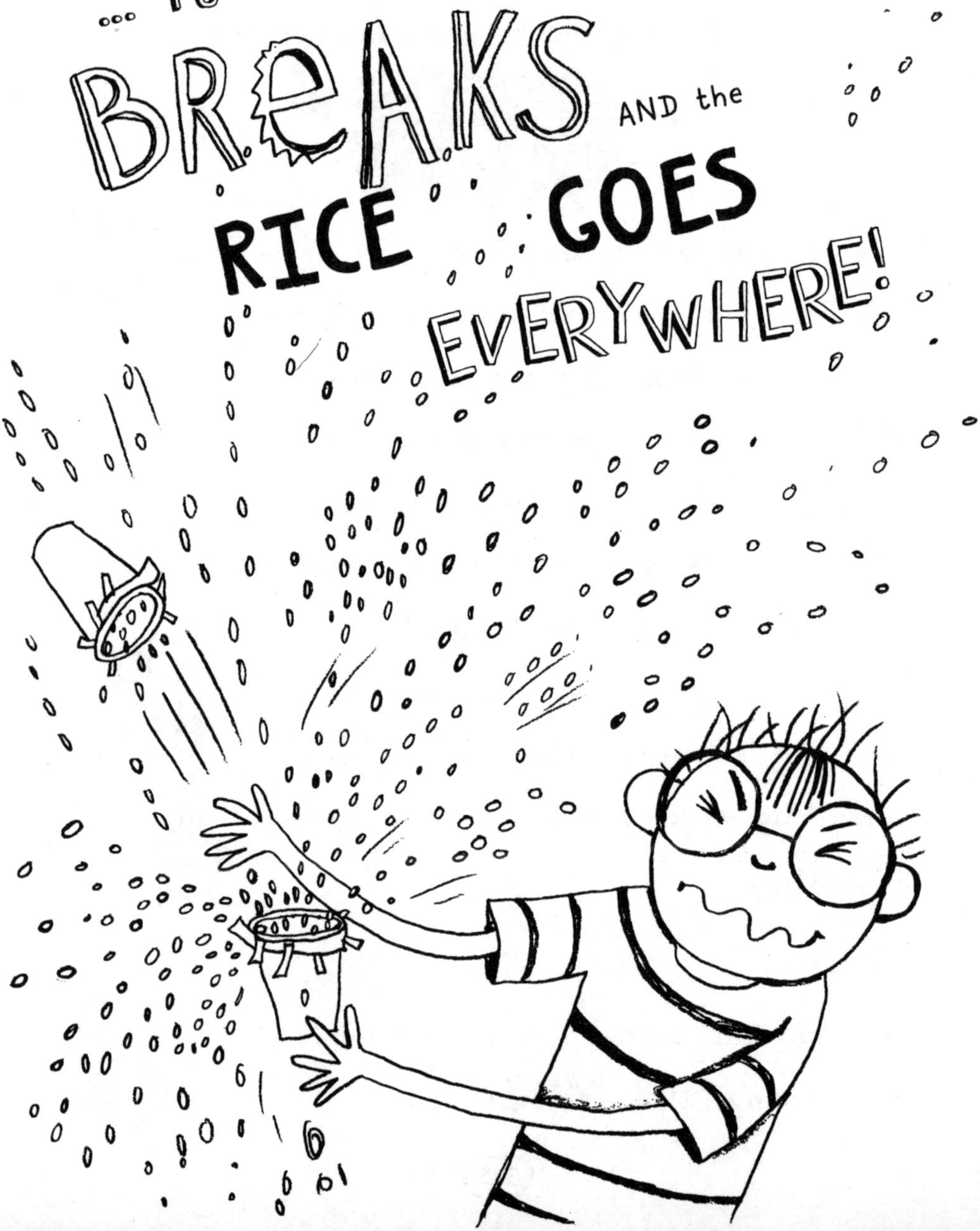
... it BREAKS AND the RICE GOES EVERYWHERE!

"Uh-oh... It broke!"
Alfie says, like it wasn't OBVIOUS.

"Sorry, Tom." Norman apologises for Alfie.

"Don't worry, it was an accident," I tell him,

just as Alfie decides to lie on the floor and shout,

"LOOK!
I'm a
RICE
ANGEL..."

"Yes you are, Alfie..." I sigh.

Then I go and get Dad.

"What happened here, then?" Dad is surprised to see all the rice.

"I'm in the BAND!"

Alfie shouts, like that explains everything.

"He's NOT. He just broke Tom's shaker. Sorry," Norman says, then Dad asks me if we can all go downstairs while he tries to clean up.

"Maybe find something LESS MESSY to do?" he adds.

Which basically means we can watch TV.

(Result.)

Everyone is happy until ...

Alfie gets up to find his bag
and he stands RIGHT in FRONT of the TV screen.

"WATCH THIS!"
Alfie says, and throws something up↑
in the air and catches it in his MOUTH.

"What are you eating, Alfie?"
Norman wants to know.

"MARSHMALLOWS!
Mini ones. Do you want some?"
(YES, WE DO!)

"Why didn't you tell us you had
MARSHMALLOWS EARLIER?" Norman wonders.

"He kind of DID," I point out as Alfie
starts sharing them out.

Catching **MARSHMALLOWS** in your mouth isn't as easy as it looks.

We agree to add mini marshmallows to our list of potential band snacks for the future.

It's only after everyone's gone home that I go upstairs and notice

SOMEONE HAS CHANGED MY SIGN.

Hmm_{mmmmm...}

Delia has been busy.

I KEEP SHOUTING
because I can't sing.

(and practising)
won't help much.
Ha! Ha!

My sister is HILARIOUS.
(Not.)

Her bedroom door might be closed, but I know Delia's in there — probably writing in her → DIARY.

I wonder what she's writing about? MAYBE she's writing about **ME?** I bet she is.

If Delia **IS** writing about me, she'll probably be saying something like **THIS.** ➡

Dear Diary,

Got up and put my on my usual sunglasses and **BLACK** clothes.

Told a WHOPPING BIG fib to Tom about Dad making pancakes. →

He didn't seem to care, which was ANNOYING.

Tom's band are coming over to practise today and that's the LAST thing I need.

If they get successful, I will be HUGELY jealous because I am NOT musical or talented in any way like Tom is. So my plan is to STOP them having any FUN at all – I'm GOOD at that.

Tom's written a stupid sign outside his room. I'm going to change it because I am HILARIOUS.

It will be really funny. Tom is not funny at all.

That's all for now.

Delia.

Next time I go into Delia's room, I might have to take a PEEK to see if she really DOES write stuff about me.

In the meantime here's a **zombie** DIARY.

Zombie rubber

Vicious pencil →

I can SEE 👀 that Dad's managed to clean up most of the rice from when Alfie **BROKE** my shaker. I'd really like to make another one to replace it, but I'll need more rice and something to put it in.

Looking around my room, the only thing I can see that might work is ... maybe a

SOCK?

I could try filling it up with some rice, but I'm not sure it would *SWISH* around inside enough, although shaking TWO socks around might look a bit fun in a band... I abandon the sock idea and go into the kitchen to find something else instead.

Shake

Shake

I'm in LUCK!

There's a half-eaten tube of crisps AND some more rice right at the ➔ BACK of the kitchen cupboard. I empty the crisps into a bowl, then eat some NOW and save the rest for later (although there's not many left).

The REALLY hard part is trying to POUR the rice into the tube. Some of it SPILLS on to the floor. So I stand on a chair, which helps (a little), and I don't fill it up <u>too</u> much.

Then I take the tube and go back to my room where I doodle on a piece of paper and STICK it to the outside of the tube. I use LOADS of sticky tape to SEAL up the lid so it's **super** tight and (hopefully) Alfie-proof.

*See page 256 on how to make a shaker.

Mum told me she wanted to hear our new song when she came back. So I try out my shaker and sing a bit of The **BISCUIT** Song, which sounds pretty good if you ask me.

I think Mum and Dad will be SUPER impressed with all the CREATIVE things I've been doing today.

I can't WAIT to show them.

It will be a NICE BIG SURPRISE

Shake
Shake
Shake
Shake
Shake

... for BOTH of them.

More
rice...
(Not cooked.)

(123)

"LOOK what I made!" I tell Mum and Dad
while showing them my NEW shaker.

"You made a bit of a MESS too, Tom,"
Mum says and points to the kitchen worktop

(which I admit does have some rice around it).

I try to distract them by demonstrating
the different SOUNDS my shaker makes.

"If you do it like THIS slowly, it sounds like

it's RAINING... Listen!"

Swish Swish Swish Swish Swish

"That DOES sound like RAIN," Dad agrees.

 (My distraction PLAN seems to be working, so I do it some more.)

"Do you want to hear a bit of the song **DOGZOMBIES** have been working on?" I ask.

"Why not?" Dad says.

 "We'd love to!" adds Mum.

Now I have to try and remember it.

"It's about BISCUITS," I explain.

"And goes something like THIS."

Shake Shake Shake Shake Shake

The **BISCUIT** Song

THE BISCUIT SONG
By DOGZOMBIES

Dog biscu←

Biscuits here
  Biscuits there
Eat a biscuit everywhere
Crunchy biscuits
  Custard creams
      Biscuits in your biscuit dreams
Shortbread biscuits
  Ginger nuts
Jammy biscuits to pick you up
Chocolate cookies
    Chocolate chips
  Melted chocolate on your lips
  Oaty crumbles
Florentine
  Those biscuits on the plate are mine

(Chorus)

Say YEAH! YEAH!

Move your biscuit FEET

Say YEAH! YEAH!

To the biscuit beat

Say YEAH! YEAH!

It's a biscuit treat

Biscuits plain and biscuits sweet

Caramel is soft and yummy

Love a wafer in my tummy

Chocolate biscuits are the best

Chocolate biscuits on my vest

Eat a biscuit up a tree

See a biscuit factory

Home-made biscuits – very nice

Biscuits hot and biscuits iced

(Repeat Chorus)

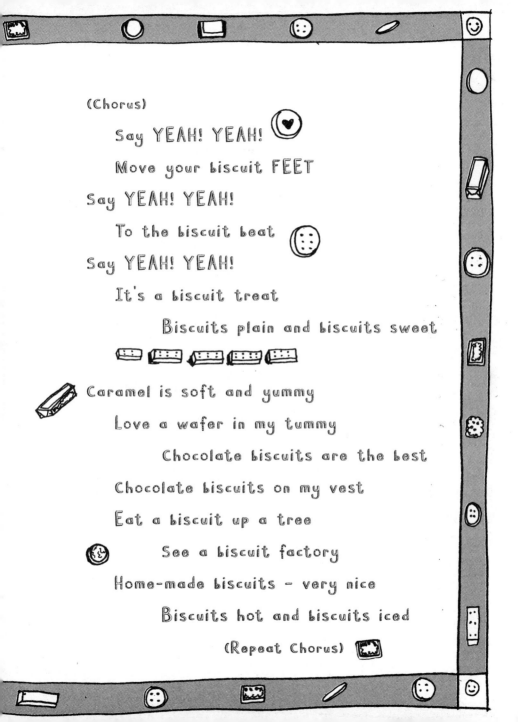

Mum and Dad give me a round of applause when I'm finished.

 "Well done, Tom. Your shaker REALLY does sound like RAIN, doesn't it?" Dad says again.

"Kind of," I agree, when I spot it IS raining now. I'm about to tell Dad when Mum says,

"Do you want to see what I bought, then?" Which is FAR more interesting than the weather.

 "I had a great time with Mavis, and I've got EVERYONE a TREAT!"

"Tea lights?" Dad asks.

 "Why do you keep asking about tea lights?" Mum wants to know.

(She's got a point.)

"I went to a great CAFE. They don't sell tea lights there, but they DO sell these cakes." Mum puts four cakes shaped like small houses on to a plate.

"Aren't they lovely? They reminded me of your shed, Frank," Mum says.

 "They're NICER than Dad's shed. He's got a hole in the roof for a start!" I point out.

"I'm going to get it fixed properly. But the bin liners are working for now. As long as it doesn't RAIN TOO HARD, it should be OK."

This seems like a good time to tell Dad, "It is raining - a LOT."

He runs off in a panic.

I turn my attention back to the treats.

"As Dad's gone, can I have his cake as well?" I ask Mum, because I can't decide which one is the nicest (or biggest).

"Nice try, Tom – you can have ONE. Didn't Dad bring you some biscuits for your band practice?"

I would answer, but my mouth is TOO FULL of CAKE. (It's delicious – if a bit small.)

While I'm enjoying the icing, I take a fork and POKE a HOLE into the roof of another cake.

"It looks a lot more like Dad's shed NOW," I tell Mum, who laughs. Then she asks about Delia.

"Is she in? I want to save her some cake – without a hole in the roof!"

"She's up in her room, probably writing things in her DIARY," I say, still eating.

 "Delia has a DIARY? How do you know – have you been snooping in her room?"

"I accidentally saw her writing in it – from a BIG distance," I quickly explain.

"Maybe I'll take her cake up to her then, just to make sure she's all right."

(Mum wants to SEE Delia's DIARY, I can tell.)

While she's gone I pick a bit more icing OFF Dad's cake and EAT it – he won't notice.

I'll just say the roof hole got bigger, that's all.

Mmmmm

I'm enjoying the **EXTRA** icing when I think I
can hear Dad calling my name.

TOM!

I go to the kitchen door and look out to his shed.
It's RAINING quite hard now, and I can SEE
Dad's climbed up the ladder and is *LEANING*
over the shed ROOF.
He's WAVING at me, so I WAVE back.

Dad keeps waving and calls me again.

Tom!

"Hi, Dad!" I say and
wave some more.

"Tom, can you PLEASE
come HERE!" Dad shouts.

It's raining a LOT now
and I don't want to get wet, so I shout,

"Do I HAVE to?"

YES!

(Dad wants me to come out.)

And BRING some BIN LINERS! he adds.

Dad's too far away to hear me GROAN, but I manage to find a ROLL and put them ON my head to keep me DRY. I pass them up to Dad, who says,

"Thanks, Tom. It was an emergency."

I take shelter in the shed and I can hear Dad hammering and trying to FIX the leak.

"I'm coming down now!" he shouts and joins me in the shed.

"I think I stopped the leak just in time," Dad says just as the water starts dripping again – right on to his HEAD.

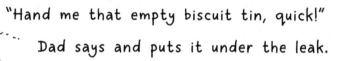

"Hand me that empty biscuit tin, quick!" Dad says and puts it under the leak.

I can't BELIEVE that Dad's EATEN the rest of the **BISCUITS!**

"It's a different tin, Tom – an old one," he tells me, but I'm NOT so sure.

Once we're back in the house, Dad starts looking for people who can fix roofs and I take the opportunity to make the hole on Dad's cake a little BIGGER by pinching a bit more of the corner ...

... only **M**um sees me this time.

Tom! No more nibbling.

When I head back upstairs, I walk past
Delia's room. Her door's SHUT, so I can't see if
she's WRITING in her DIARY.

I knock on her door to check that she's there.

WHAT?

"Nothing," I reply, which annoys her.

Go away,
Tom.

I'm not going to be able to sneak the

ROCK WEEKLYS back now. I hide them under
my bed wrapped up in a jumper. They should be
SAFE enough there for a while.

I find MORE rice LURKING around
that I sweep up into my hand. I'm about
to put it into the bin when I get a much better
idea instead...

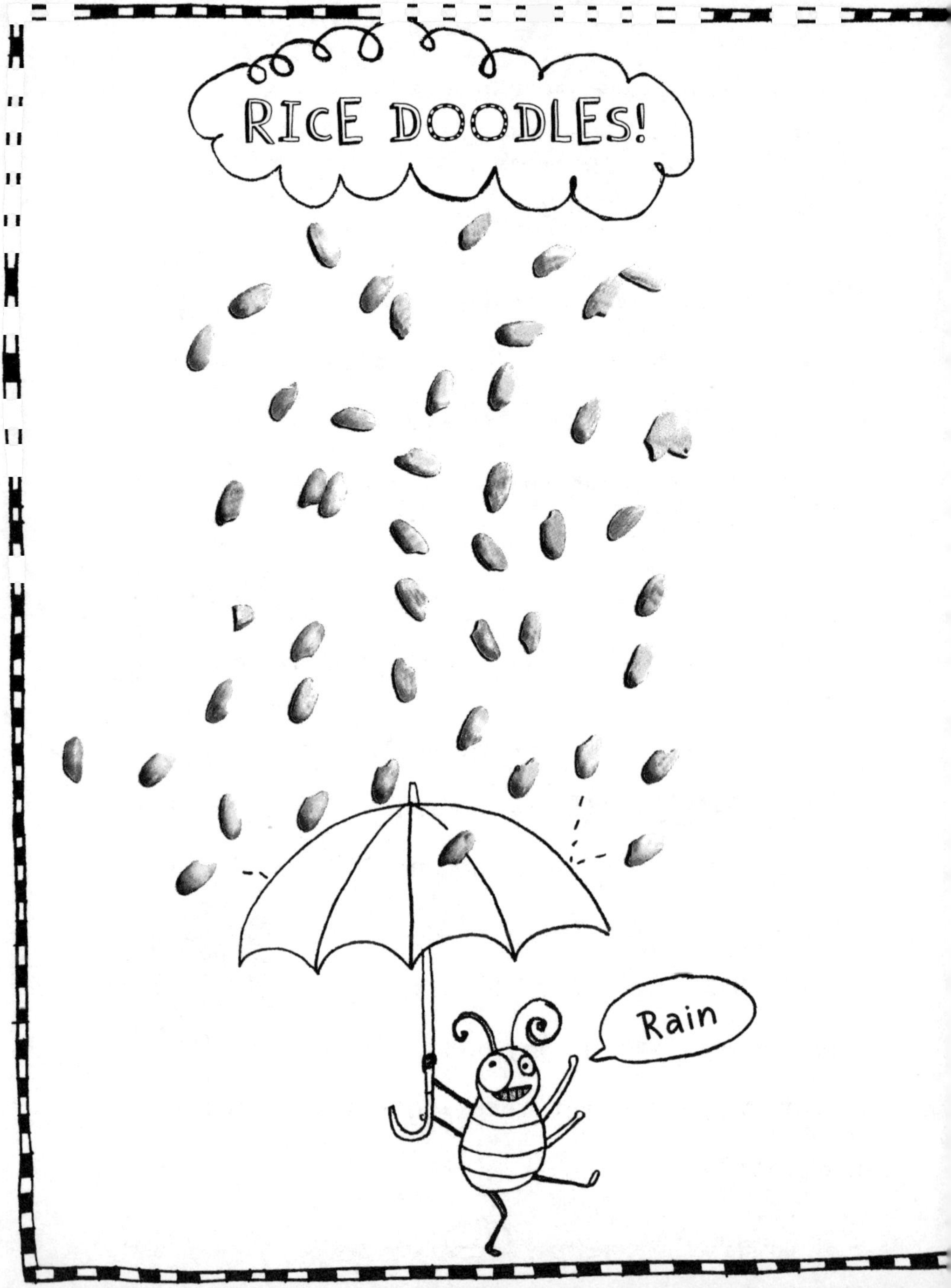
RICE DOODLES!
Rain

In the morning, I hear Delia go out EARLY. THIS is my chance to put the **ROCK WEEKLYS** back in her room. I quickly unwrap them from my jumper. They're a bit scrunched up, but that doesn't matter.

I check that Delia <u>has</u> actually gone, taking the magazines with me.

"Delia? Deeelia? Deeeelliaa!" I call out and get no answer, so I know it's SAFE to go in.

I try to be as **FAST** as I can and put them back where I found them. Delia has MOVED things around...

... but I try my BEST to make it look like I haven't been snooping at ALL.

I put the **ROCK WEEKLYS** on top of each other on her shelf when I suddenly SPOT DELIA'S DIARY — and it's OPEN.

It's saying, READ ME! READ ME!

I HAVE to take a sneaky peek now.

I turn the first few pages and I can't BELIEVE WHAT I'm reading.

Delia's DIARY is ...

REALLY BORING

Yawn...

It's SO DULL, if I read it before bedtime it would put me to sleep. There's NOTHING interesting at ALL, just lists of things. I put it back under the ROCK WEEKLYS where I found it.

I don't want to be late for school, so I slip out of her bedroom before anyone SEES ME.

When I meet up with Derek, I tell him all about the DIARY.

"I read Delia's DIARY."

"Were you in it?" he asks.

"I didn't read that much because it was SO DULL - really boring."

 "I had a DIARY once, but I kept forgetting to write in it."

 "I might start writing a DIARY. I'm sure The Wrinklies have given me one. I could put all the funny things that happen to me in it. There's always something."

 "I'd read your DIARY," Derek tells me.

 "It would be a lot more interesting than Delia's DIARY, that's for sure."

My DIARY would be EXTRA BIG.

(Like this...) ➜

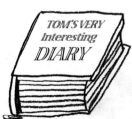

TOM'S VERY
Interesting
DIARY

I'm in class and busy thinking about WHAT $I'\underline{d}$
write in a DIARY if I had one when Marcus says,
"Hey, Tom, look at my drawing."
I don't have much choice as he's waving it at me.

 "I give up – what is it?"

"It's a DOG, of course," he tells me.

"It's got a very small head for a dog, or a
very BIG body," I point out.

(See?) →

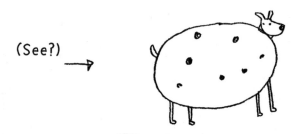

"The dog's just eaten a lot. I'll do something else, then. What shall I draw? I can draw ANYTHING."

"ANYTHING?" AMY and I both say at the same time.

"Yes, ANYTHING... Mostly anything."

We take that as a CHALLENGE and start asking Marcus to draw a few different things.

So far we've asked him for:

A cat with a hat

A horse

A chicken

An elephant

A Bush Baby

(that's hard)

A fox

A HAIRY LEG!

I'm not sure he heard everything we said.

"SEE, I told you I'm good at drawing!"

Marcus says, sounding quite SMUG.

"You are, even if you did draw a horse

with a BUSHY tail and a hairy egg," I tell him.

"Your drawings are VERY entertaining,"

AMY laughs.

"I know, thank you," Marcus says, then we all

have to get out our books *quickly* as Mr Fullerman

is on the move.

Well done, you three

Good reading.

The class is so QUIET I can hear my stomach

rumbling. The lesson before lunch is the hardest if

you're really hungry (like I am).

There are some nice FOOD smells wafting up from the lunch hall, which is making my stomach grumble even MORE.

Rumble Rumble Rumble Rumble Rumble

EVERYONE can hear it rumble.

"Was that your stomach?" AMY asks me.

Rumble Rumble Rumble

"Maybe," I say and shift around a bit, which doesn't help much.

"SSShhhhhh, Tom. I'm trying to read," Marcus mutters.

"I can't help it. I'm hungry."

It's a while before lunch, so to stop my stomach grumbling so much, I have a quick check in my bag to see if there's anything to eat hiding in there.

YES!

I think I've found something.

It's an OLD packet of cheesy crackers.
It feels a bit **CRUNChED** up, but THIS is an

EMERGENCY.

Yes to what?

Marcus wants to know.

"Nothing." I get out my pencil case and hide the crackers behind it so he can't see what I've got.

"You're HIDING something!" Marcus says.

"No I'm not."

"What have you got?"

Marcus is so NOSEY.

"Mind your own beeswax," I tell him.

"Why have you got BEESWAX? Let me see!"

"I don't have BEESWAX — it means 'mind your own business'. I haven't got anything," I tell him again as my stomach keeps **rumbling.**

(148)

Beady eye alert!

Mr Fullerman is LOOKING at us now and
wondering what we're talking about. It's going
to be IMPOSSIBLE to eat anything without being
caught. I shove the crackers up my sweatshirt, then

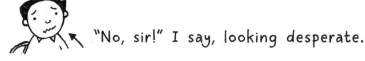

put my hand up to ask Mr Fullerman
if I can go to the toilet.

(Good plan.)

Rumble
Rumble

"It's not long until lunch,
Tom. Can't you wait?"

"No, sir!" I say, looking desperate.

"Be QUICK, then..." Mr Fullerman tells me as
I walk past, trying hard not to rustle the crackers
or let them fall out of my sweatshirt.

As soon as I'm outside I shove a WHOLE
handful of crackers into my mouth really quickly.

I manage to SCOFF even more as I walk
towards the toilet.

I'm feeling quite pleased with myself
when out of NOWHERE ...
MRS NAP suddenly appears.

"Hello, Tom. Where are you off to, then?"
she wants to know. I point to the
toilet so I don't have to talk.
"Actually, you're just the person I want to see."

(Huh? I keep quiet.)
"I need some KEEN singers for our CHOIR this year.
We're entering a competition, which will be so much
FUN."

 (Uh-oh.)

 "You're in a BAND and you SING,
don't you?"

$\mathcal{I}$ nod again, chewing quietly.

"$\mathcal{SO}$ you'll come and join us...
WON'T YOU, TOM?"

"Mmmmmmmmmm."

(I like singing, but I'm not keen on all the lunchtime practising, and I'm already in **DOGZOMBIES**.)

"Mmmmmmmy Fffffank." I try and talk but I can't.

"GREAT – I'll put your name down. It's
going to be very exciting as we're
playing with the Recycled Orchestra too!"

(Things are just getting worse.)

$\mathcal{M}$r $\mathcal{F}$ullerman opens the classroom door to find
out why Mrs Nap is talking to me.

"Is everything OK, Mrs Nap?"

"It's more than OK, Mr Fullerman. Tom
has just agreed to join the school choir!"

"WELL DONE, Tom, that's great news. Come back to class now. There seem to be a LOT of children who suddenly need the toilet."

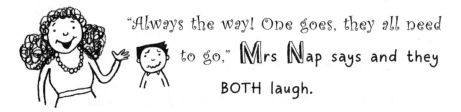

"Always the way! One goes, they all need to go," Mrs Nap says and they BOTH laugh.

I do the BEST cheery face I can manage while hiding what's left of my crackers.

I sit back at my desk and straight away Marcus looks at me and says, "What's that under your sweatshirt?" Then he PRODS me and I go CRUNCH.

"It's nothing," I tell him.

Then AMY tells me I smell of crisps.

"I KNEW it! Let's have some," Marcus says.

"I don't have any left – and they aren't crisps.
AND Mr Fullerman is coming over, so SHHH."
I tell them, hoping Marcus will keep quiet.

 **"Tom, you know there's no EATING
in class,"** Mr Fullerman says.

"SIR?"

I pretend to have NO idea what he means.
Then he points to the floor and the trail of cracker
crumbs that leads all the way up to my desk.
"Oh. Whoops."

Mr Fullerman asks me to stay behind
after class ...

... to sweep up the crumbs.

(I use the time to try and THINK up some excuses for NOT being in the *choir.*)

So far I've thought of these...

Space for another idea

Thanks to Mum, there is NO WAY I can get out of being in the *choir* now. She found the competition form in my bag and signed it straight away.

All done!

Oh...

"The form says the Recycled Orchestra needs shoeboxes urgently, and I've got LOADS. Why don't I help you take them to school, and we can hand in your form as well," Mum tells me.

"Great..." I say, not very enthusiastically, as I'd been planning on accidentally leaving it behind.

So this morning I'm walking to school with Derek, Mum and LOTS of shoeboxes.

"How many pairs of shoes have you got?" Derek asks me.

"Not many – these are Mum's," I tell him.

"Most of them aren't mine."

(They are.)

When we get to school, the first person we see is Mrs Nap and Mum calls out, "HELLO, Mrs Nap!" really loudly.

"See you later," Derek says and leaves me to it. I have to STAY and listen to Mum and Mrs Nap chit-chatting about the school *choir* and ME for what seems like AGES. (Groan.)

"I know Tom forgets his forms, so we've brought in the *choir* one together. The competition sounds GREAT!"

Mrs Nap smiles and says, "Would you be free to come with us and help out, Mrs Gates? We really need more parents around."

Normally Mum's too busy when it comes to things like this, so I'm not worried.

Only THIS TIME she says,
"YES, of course – I'd LOVE to come along and help out."

"That's great, Mrs Gates. Thank you so MUCH!"

"But, but, but!" I splutter.

Mum completely ignores me and carries on talking as if I'm NOT even there.

"Tom's always liked singing. He used to sing ALL the time when he was little. He'd sit singing AWAY for HOURS, even when he was on the..."

"Mum! No one wants to hear THAT!"

"We do!" Florence and AMY

say as they walk past.

"On the POTTY! Oh! I think I'm embarrassing Tom. I'd better go. Unless you need help taking in the shoeboxes?"

"No, I'm fine," I mutter.

Mrs Nap takes some boxes from Mum while I go into school quickly before she can say ANYTHING else embarrassing.

BYE, Tommy Tom-Tom!

Too late.

Tommy Tom-Tom!

Ha!

When Mr Fullerman sees HOW many boxes I've brought in he wants me to take them down to the recycling drop-off point right away. Julia Morton comes with me as she's taking a note to the office.

"Does your mum always call you Tommy Tom-Tom?" is the first thing she asks me.

"No – just Tom. I don't know why she said that." We leave the shoeboxes at the recycling point and Julia goes to the office.
I take the opportunity to have a look at what else is there.

There are all kinds of pots, bottles and cardboard tubes. I notice there's a HAT on the floor too, so I pick it up and put it into the box next to the shoeboxes.

That hat would make a VERY good drum, I think. I'll look out for it when the Recycled Orchestra is playing.

I'm feeling quite pleased with myself for being helpful when Julia comes back and says, "Come on, Tommy Tom-Tom! Let's get back to class."

"Just 'Tom' is fine, Julia."

Sigh...

Shame – I like Tommy Tom-Tom.

Back in class, Mr Fullerman is doing a science lesson with us, and <u>amazingly</u> I finish my worksheet EARLY. ☺

Looking around the class, I'm not the only one (AMY has too). So Mr Fullerman says we can spend the rest of the lesson READING or doodling.

(He didn't really say that, but it's what I'm doing.)

Since Marcus decided he is an EXPERT on drawing ...

... he keeps telling me what I'm about to draw.

"I know what that is. You're drawing Mr Fullerman, aren't you?"

 "**A**ctually, Marcus, it's NOT **M**r **F**ullerman."

"Yes, it is, I can tell."

"No, it's not..." I say. (This is a good game.)

"It is **M**r **F**ullerman – you always draw him like that."

"No, you're wrong..."

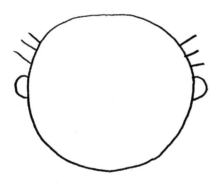

(I carry on drawing to show him what it is.)

"It's a BEAR holding a tray with a CAKE," I tell Marcus.

"You just CHANGED it!"

"No, I didn't. Look, I'll do another one. See if you can guess right this time," I tell him. This is FUN.

"It's one of your **ROBOTS,**"

Marcus says, sounding VERY confident.

"You couldn't be more wrong..."

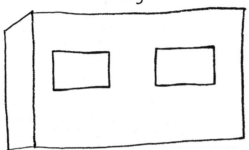

"It's a BUILDING, then – with windows."

 (Marcus is getting frustrated.)

"Guess again." I keep drawing.

"I don't know ... YET," he says.

So I finish the doodle off.

"It's a FLY-eating plant, of COURSE!
Not a **ROBOT**."

"You just CHANGED the drawing again, didn't you?"

"No. What makes you think that? This time I'm going to make it SO EASY for you," I say and start to draw...

"THAT'S a **MONSTER** doodle!" Marcus says.

"Are you sure? It might not be. Keep watching..." I tell him.

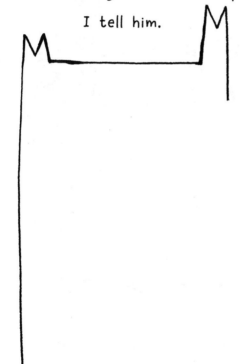

"You're cheating!" Marcus says. "Do another one – I'll get it this time."

(He won't.)

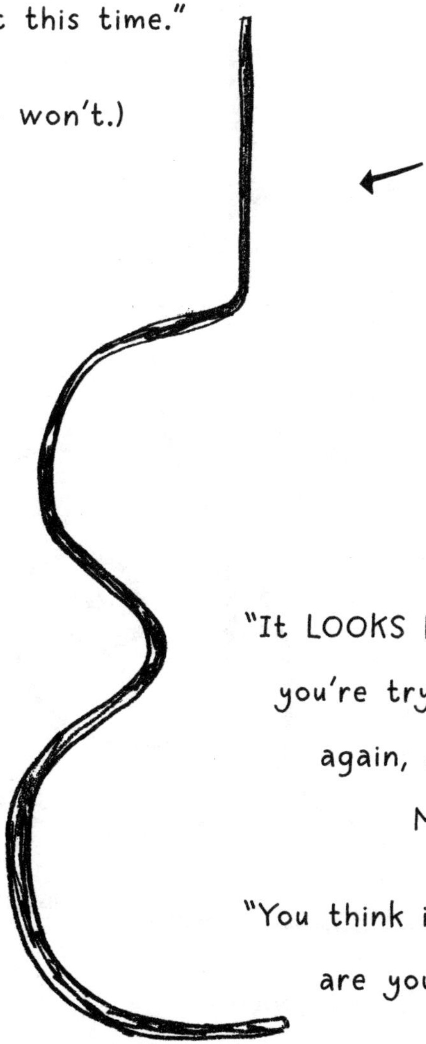

← I draw this.

"It LOOKS like a guitar, but you're trying to trick me again, aren't you?" Marcus says.

"You think it's a GUITAR ... are you SURE?" I say.

"No."

 "It's a smiling SNAIL!"

(Of course it is.)

Marcus looks grumpy, so I give him one last chance to tell me what I'm drawing...

"You **MUST** know what this is!"

 "Is it **ME?**" Marcus wonders.

"Not really..."

(I keep drawing to show him.)

"It's a PIE..."

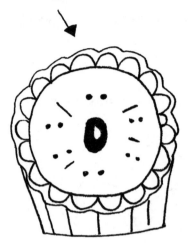

"Or a DOG..."

"OR a long-legged BUG on a unicycle..."

I could play this game ALL DAY!

I do a few more for Marcus so he can draw on his OWN face, which makes him VERY confused.

MR
Keen

Some pictures to try out

Here's some **MORE.**

slower

delia

𝔻oodling fills up my whole day.

It takes my mind off other things that are coming up.

The next day we have an assembly, and Mr Keen, our headmaster, wants to congratulate some kids on...

Winning the netball tournament. Well done to the whole team.

They stand up slowly and we all have to clap.

"There were only three teams playing. It wasn't a big tournament," Solid tells me.

Which sounds about right for our school. Then Mrs Nap says she has news about the *choir* COMPETITION.

(Uh-oh.)

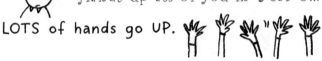

"Hands up all of you in Year 5..."

LOTS of hands go UP.

I put mine halfway up while I wait to hear what else she's going to say.

"Keep them up if you LOVE singing and want to take part in this year's CHOIR COMPETITION."

Most of the hands go down, including mine. I'm hoping Mrs Nap will forget me completely.

Then AMY says, "Hey, Tom – Mrs Nap is looking at you. Are YOU in the *choir*, then?"

"No, I'm definitely NOT. She must be looking at someone else," I tell AMY.

"Come on, Tom," says Mrs Nap. "Have you forgotten? YOU'RE IN THE CHOIR! Put your hand up!"

"I forgot..." I mutter.

(There's no getting out of it now.)

Mrs Nap tries to encourage MORE children to be in the *choir*.

"This year we're being joined by Mr Sprocket's wonderful Recycled Orchestra.

So let's invite a few members up to play some of the instruments they've made from your donations of boxes, bottles and other things."

Mrs Nap makes her way to the piano as the kids set up their "instruments" to join in with her playing.

Ping
Ping

Ding Ding

Bang Bang

"Is that a plastic funnel?" Norman wonders.

"I think it is," Solid agrees. "Is that kid playing some kind of drum?"

"I think that's the hat I found," I tell them both. "IT IS the HAT!"

"It's the HAT I picked up from the floor and put in the recycling box. I knew it would make a good drum!" I say again.

"I think I'm going to join the *choir* too," Norman tells me, which is good news.

Mrs Nap finishes playing and stands up to say, "Well done for showing everyone how wonderful your recycled instruments are! I can't wait to hear you playing with the choir!" As the orchestra walk past her she NOTICES the DRUM and looks SURPRISED.

"Oh? Hang on..."

"That drum looks like a hat!"

"It is, Mrs Nap," the kid playing the drum tells her.

"It looks like MY HAT! I was wondering where it got to!"

 Mr Keen comes over.

**"Is there a problem,
Mrs Nap?"**

"I'm not sure how this happened, but my HAT has become a DRUM," she tells him.

 "I found it in the recycling box!" the kid
playing the drum says.

"I wonder how it got there?" Mrs Nap wants to know.

**"If it's any consolation, Mrs Nap, it
makes an excellent drum," Mr Keen says.**

Mrs Nap holds up the hat drum. "Does anyone
know how my hat ended up in the recycling box?"

Uh-oh...

I'm not going to say **anything**. I only picked
it up because it was on the floor and I was being
helpful. Solid nudges me, and so does Norman.

 "Shhhh!" I mutter.

Then MARCUS leans
forward and prods me.

"Didn't YOU find that hat, Tom?" he says.

I ignore him and start rummaging in my
pockets nervously for something to do.

 "You said you found it!" he says
again. I pull out some FLUFF from my
pocket, then whisper, "I didn't..." to try
and keep him quiet.

I notice the **FLUFF** in my hand looks a bit like a
spider, so I think QUICKLY and drop it on the floor
in front of Marcus.

"MARCUS, LOOK! Is that a SPIDER near your leg?"

(This could be a good distraction.)

Mrs Nap is still LOOKING around the hall when Marcus shouts out, →

WHERE?

WHAT SPIDER?!

Then there's a BIG BUNDLE of kids all trying to get away from my **fluff.** Which <u>stops</u> all the talk of hats and drums.

"OK, everyone – that's enough. Sit down, please. I'll be handing out the choir forms as you leave."

My **fluff** worked a treat. I quickly pick it up and put it in my pocket for another time.

It <u>could</u> come in VERY handy for other difficult situations as it does sort of look like a spider ... if you don't count its legs.

Here are some other ways I could use my new **FLUFF** SPIDER:

Protecting <u>my</u> favourite mini cereal.

Saving **D**erek a seat at lunchtime.

AMY is not bothered by the <u>spider</u> because she has spotted it's not real, but any time Marcus mentions that HAT, I'll bring out the **FLUFF** spider for sure.

Inspired by my **FLUFF** spider, I do a whole page of **FLUFF** doodles.

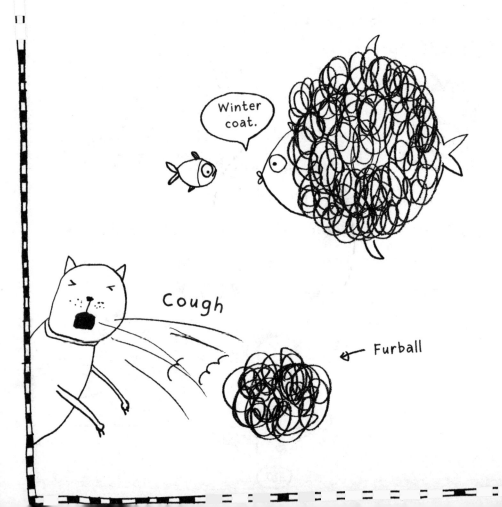

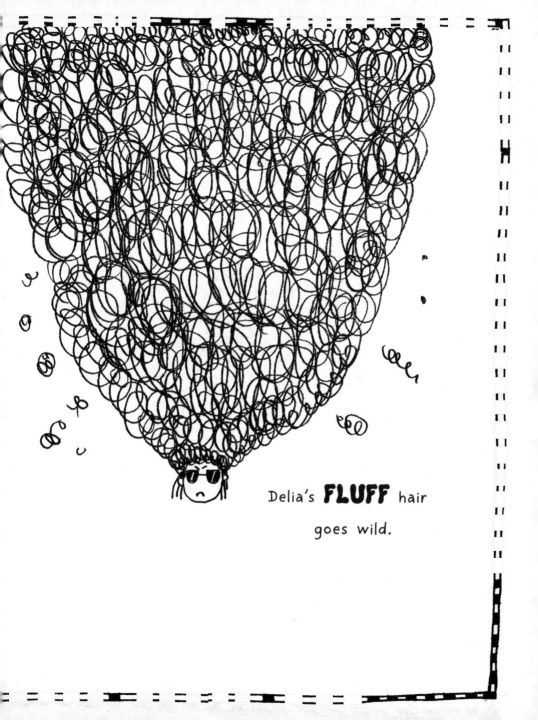

Delia's **FLUFF** hair goes wild.

Spare FLUFF for other ideas.

Marge
Simpson

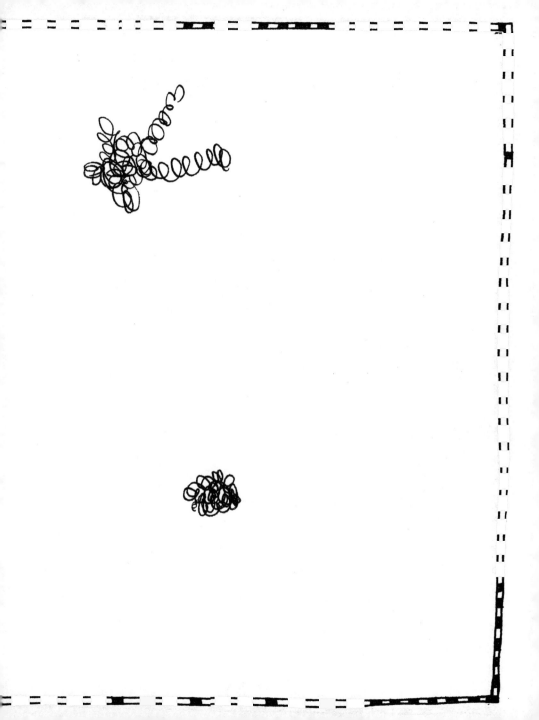

 New day - NEW plan

The Wrinklies  (my grandparents) have gone on what they said was...

> A little minibreak up a mountain. If we have time, we'll do a bungee jump too!

Mum wasn't happy about that.

"What's wrong with just staying in a nice hotel and relaxing?"

But they went anyway. So I asked Mum, "When you're really OLD - in a couple of years - will **you** do things like that?"

"What do you mean, in a COUPLE OF YEARS? I'm not THAT old!" Mum told me, shaking her head. "But, no - I won't be bungee-jumping EVER."

My other grandparents, **THE FOSSILS**, are not going on a CRAZY holiday any time soon. Though Granddad Bob has been a bit ═══ *SPEEDY* on his mobility scooter since it went in to be FIXED. ═══

W h i z z ═══

They've invited me over to have TEA with them today. If I knew what kind of tea we'd be having, it would be better. Sometimes I don't recognize anything they put on the table. It's like a GUESSING GAME.

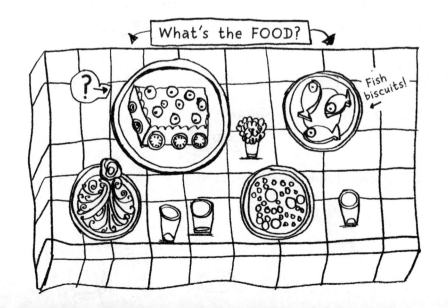

When Dad drops me off at their house he hands me a pack of FIG ROLLS.

"Here, Tom, take these with you."

"WHY?" I ask, as they're not my favourite biscuits at all.

FIG ROLLS are way —————→ → →

down ↓

on my biscuit list.

Almost under garibaldis.

"Mavis loves them. Bob, not so much, as they get stuck to his teeth," Dad tells me.

Fig teeth

"I'll treat them as EMERGENCY biscuits," I say.

YUCK

THE FOSSILS are delighted with the fig rolls, Thank you

How nice (even Granddad Bob).

"We'll take them with us!" Granny tells me, which is confusing as I thought we were staying HERE.

"We're going to see **Teacup Tony** at the LEAFY GREEN OLD FOLKS' HOME. We'll head over THERE as we've got a surprise for him."

"What kind of a surprise?" I wonder.

"We've got a portable record player and we've bought some of **Tony's** old albums for him to hear!"

Which is nice but there's NO mention of TEA at all.

Or, even more importantly, WHEN we're having it. (It could be fig rolls for me after all.)

 Yuck.

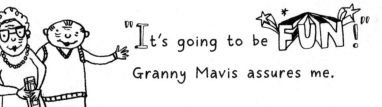

"It's going to be **FUN**!" Granny Mavis assures me.

"OK," I say, but I'm slightly worried because the LEAFY GREEN OLD FOLKS' HOME isn't always as FUN as they're making it out to be.

Then Granny Mavis adds, "And we're going to order pizza while we're there, if that's OK with you?"

"LET'S GO, I'M READY!"

(That's better.)

It doesn't take us long to get there, thanks to Granddad's souped-up mobility scooter.

Whhheee

Whizz

When we arrive there's a BIG game of

BINGO* going on, but no sign of **Teacup Tony** anywhere.

Two little ducks - 22

Tickety-boo - 62

Vera tells Granny Mavis that he's having a POWER NAP. zzzz

He won two games of bingo earlier and celebrated in a VERY energetic way. So he's a bit tired now.

Yippee!

*See more about bingo on page 260.

It gives us a chance to set up the record player and put out his albums for when he wakes up.

"I had no idea **Tony** had made so many," Vera says, looking impressed.

"I like this one – it's a favourite. Let's put it on!" Granddad suggests. "Can you do that, Tom?"

"I can!"

Thanks to **D**erek's dad, who's got a record player, I know exactly what to do. I put on **"A Nice Cup of Tea"** very carefully, which reminds me about <u>my</u> TEA.

"Is anyone else HUNGRY yet?"

I ask hopefully, because I am.

THE FOSSILS are already dancing, so I'm guessing

I'm going to have to wait, or eat the FIG ROLLS.

(Though I'm not that desperate, YET.)

I try dropping a few more HINTS instead.

"This record is ROUND

like a PIZZA," I say.

"It is!" Granddad smiles

and keeps swaying.

While I'm thinking of

what to say NEXT, the lady

calling the BINGO numbers comes to see us.

"Hello! Can I ask you a favour about the

music you're playing?" she asks.

"We'll turn it down straight away!

It's Teacup Tony. We wanted him

to hear it. Sorry!" Granny apologizes.

NO! We want you to TURN it UP so all the [BINGO] players can hear! They're loving **"A Nice Cup Of Tea"!**

 Which is unexpected, 🙂 AND so is the ⚡ sudden ⚡ appearance of

TEACUP TONY, →

Hello!

who's already playing the spoons.

"I thought I recognized THAT song – it WOKE me UP! ♪ 'A nice cup of tea!'" ♪ he sings.

I turn up the record and we listen to the song again at ⚡ **FULL BLAST** so everyone can hear it – even Vera.

This is a nice tune!

Just in case they've forgotten, I remind that...

"Listening to music makes me REALLY HUNGRY!"

Finally, they AGREE! Granny Mavis

YES!

takes our pizza orders which makes

me VERY HAPPY!

Yum —

Teacup Tony is pretty pleased

as well.

Pizzas!

While we're waiting for them

to be delivered, we put on

more of Tony's album*.

"It's so NICE of you to bring them," he says.

"It's our PLEASURE!" Granddad Bob smiles.

"Have I ever told you about the time the band and

I went on tour with a circus, a motorcycle and a

small dog?" Tony asks us 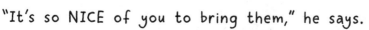 (He hasn't.)

We're still listening when the pizzas arrive.

*See page 258 for Tony's albums.

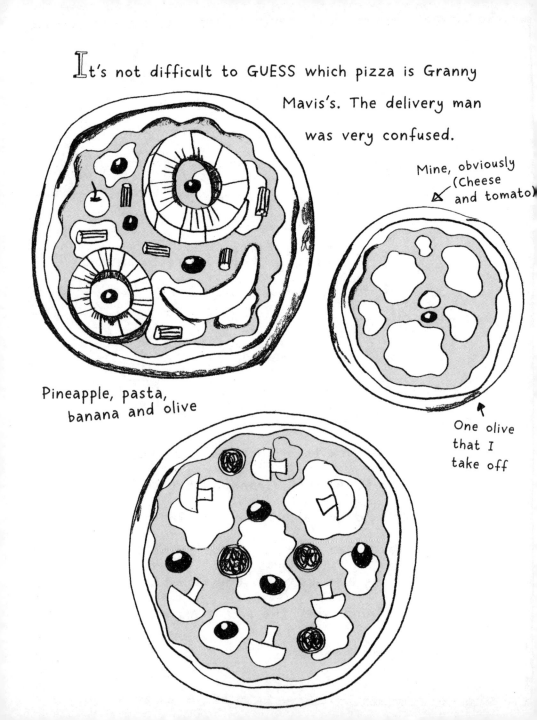

It's not difficult to GUESS which pizza is Granny Mavis's. The delivery man was very confused.

Mine, obviously (Cheese and tomato)

Pineapple, pasta, banana and olive

One olive that I take off

Here are some pizzas for more unusual toppings.

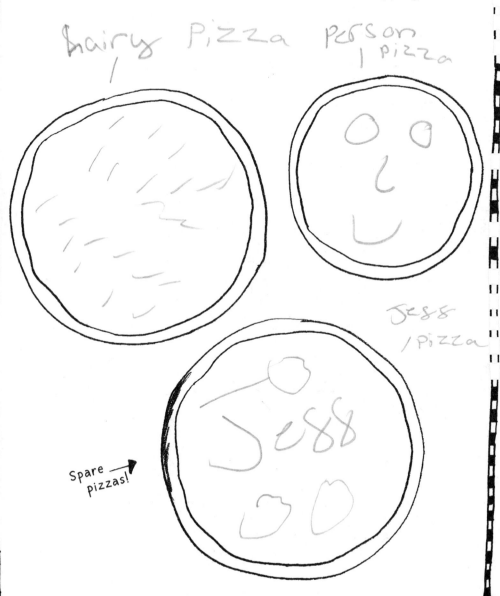

hairy Pizza

Person
1 pizza

Jess
1 pizza

Spare → Pizzas!

Jess

When I get home, Mum wants to know ALL about my visit. "How was it?"

"A lot more FUN than I thought it would be. They brought a RECORD PLAYER for **Teacup Tony** and played all his albums," I tell her.

"Was the pizza good?" Mum asks.

"How did you know I had pizza?"

"It's still on your sweatshirt, and your face, so it must have been NICE!"

(Whoops.)

To take her mind off the mess, I let Mum know that I'm going to be keeping a DIARY with drawings in it. **"Teacup Tony** told me his stories about being in a band, so I have lots to write about."

"Nice stories, I hope?" Mum asks me, then wipes my face.

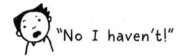

"**M**um! My DIARY will have WAY more interesting things in it than Delia's DIARY!" I manage to add.

The trouble with Delia is she has a WAY of turning up at the WRONG TIME, like RIGHT NOW.

"**TOM!** I <u>know</u> you've been taking my magazines AND reading my DIARY."

"No I haven't!"

"<u>Y</u>es, you have."

"Why would I want to read your BORING diary full of LISTS?" (Whoops.)

"I KNEW it. Don't read my DIARY, Tom, OK?"

"Well don't read <u>MY</u> DIARY either."

"You don't have a DIARY — and even if you did, I wouldn't read it," Delia tells me, then stomps OFF in a huff.

"Don't do it again, Tom," Mum says, like it was my fault Delia left it OPEN.

When I get back to my room, Delia has DUMPED a pile of ROCK WEEKLYS outside my DOOR. "What's she up to NOW?" I wonder. There's a note on top that says,

At first I think it's quite nice of Delia to let me have them. But they're only the ones I soaked with paint water. She's right - they are a MESS. The one I REALLY want is the ROCK WEEKLY with DUDE3 inside.

Tom
These are a MESS! Keep them.

I'm going to give them back and ASK her for the DUDE3 copy instead. You never know - she might let me have it.

(It's a plan.)

But she's not in her room, so I do a *QUICK SWAP,* and take the one I want.

Then I spot Delia's DIARY, AND IT'S OPEN AGAIN.

I'm NOT going to read it, because it's BORING.

But then I SEE my NAME on a page.

Delia has been writing about ME.

So I HAVE to read it now.

Dear Diary,

I have so many things to write about today,
I don't know where to start!
   Firstly, I have a VERY

BIG SECRET,

and keeping it to myself isn't going to be

easy. The ONE person I can't tell is my little

brother, <u>TOM,</u> who will BLAB to everyone.

So <u>HE</u> mustn't know that I've been having

secret drum lessons.

YES, I play the DRUMS!

Even Mum and Dad think I've been going round to Avril's house, but REALLY I've been practising and taking lessons.

It's been SO ANNOYING when <u>Tom</u> and his band practise at home, and TERRIBLE listening to them make good songs sound really BAD. <u>Tom</u> can be VERY annoying. Let me write that again, only bigger...

TOM IS VERY ANNOYING.

It's true. I can't let Tom know that I went for an audition to be in a music video as the drummer, AND I've just found out

I GOT THE JOB!

I am VERY excited.

But nobody can find out, because the band that's making the video is VERY famous. It's been really hard keeping it all a secret.

Tom would go CRAZY if he knew who it was, which is why he must NEVER know EVER. I'm going to have to keep the name of the band ALL to myself for a while longer at least. I could write it in my diary?

Maybe I will.

WHOOOAAAH!

I wasn't expecting **THAT.** This is a **LOT** more interesting than BEFORE. Delia plays the drums? She's going to be in a music video?

MY GRUMPY SISTER DELIA?

I really want to know who the band is – so I keep reading.

I had to STOP writing because <u>Tom</u> has been SNOOPING around my room, and taking my collection of <u>ROCK WEEKLYS</u>.

I've told him not to, but he keeps ON doing it. He tells me with a STRAIGHT face that he hasn't looked in my DIARY.
  BUT I <u>know</u> he has. In fact, he's probably reading it RIGHT NOW.

HELLO, TOM!

YES I know you have been snooping in my room! SO you'll never guess what I've done?

(Hold on tight...)

My WHOLE DIARY (yes, this one)

is covered in a VERY special DUST.

So every time you touch my diary, the

DUST will get on your hands.

 You can't SEE it, but it's there.

The dust will turn your fingers

PURPLE.

You won't be able to WASH it off for a

week, maybe MORE (depending on how nosey

you've been).

Also, before you go BLABBING to everyone that I'm a drummer and in a music video, I made that UP to get your attention and keep you reading for longer, so your fingers are going to be REALLY purple now — maybe not straight away, as the dust takes a while to work.

LET THIS BE A LESSON FOR YOU! NO SNOOPING in other people's rooms or private diaries.

I look forward to seeing your purple fingers. If you tell Mum and Dad, they'll be cross with YOU.

Love Delia x x

HUH?
Oh NO!

I don't want
purple fingers!

I DROP the DIARY **FAST** and go to wash
my hands.

I don't want to RISK anyone seeing my fingers GO
purple - especially <u>NOT</u> Delia.

I need to think of something... *FAST!*

I put on my gloves, then get ready for school.
Downstairs at breakfast, Dad says,

"Tom, why are you wearing gloves? It's not COLD."

"Um... No reason, I just want to,"
I tell Dad.

"You should take them off to eat."

"I'm FINE, thanks," I say, like it's totally normal to
wear gloves and eat cereal.
When Delia comes in, she looks at my GLOVES
and comes to sit NEXT to me.

(A bit too close for my liking.)
I keep eating as calmly as I can.

"So, Tom, why are you wearing
GLOVES, then?"

"I asked him the same question."

"Because I want to - what's the BIG deal? And can you give me some S P A C E, please?" I ask Delia.

"Have you been reading my DIARY by any chance ... AGAIN?" she wants to know.

"NO!" I say and eat faster, so I can LEAVE quickly.

(This isn't going well.)

Delia moves even CLOSER.
"Because if you have, I WILL FIND OUT, thanks to the SPECIAL dust I've put ALL over the pages. Anyone who's been reading it will have ... purple fingers. AND THEN - THEY WILL DROP OFF."

I gulp. "Really?"

"YES, REALLY."

I'm trying to stay CALM and NOT PANIC,

but this news is

TOO MUCH.

"OK, I read your DIARY!" I shout.

"I don't want my fingers to drop off."

"I KNOW you read it, Tom – you have to STOP

sneaking around my ROOM, doesn't he, Dad?"

Delia is not happy at all.

"Come on, Tom, have you been reading her DIARY?"

"Maybe just a little bit – not much."

"Anything interesting in there?" Dad asks.

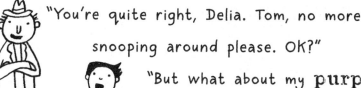

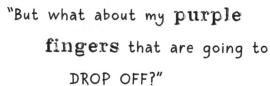

"**DAD!** You're NOT supposed to ENCOURAGE HIM - it's PRIVATE!"

"You're quite right, Delia. Tom, no more snooping around please. OK?"

"But what about my **purple fingers** that are going to DROP OFF?"

I take my gloves off to show them both.

"They still look NORMAL," I say.

"For NOW," Delia chips in.

"So they won't drop off, then?" I ask Dad.

"They might if you do it **AGAIN,**" Delia tells me.

"You two <u>really</u> need to STOP winding each other up!" Dad tells us BOTH off.

I tell Delia I WON'T read her DIARY any more and she says, "Good," and heads off to college.

I put my gloves back on - just in case.

Delia ever leaves her DIARY open again, I'll just have to be a **LOT** more careful and use EVERYTHING to protect myself when I'm reading it.

(No more **purple fingers** for me.)

Future
reading

I've been trying to (think) of ways to get Delia back for tricking me, but I haven't come up with anything YET. BLANK

Delia said she wouldn't read MY DIARY because it would be Boring. But I have LOADS of interesting things to write about, especially as the *choir* COMPETITION is coming up.

So THAT'S NOT TRUE. My diary is going to be PACKED full of excellent stuff. And if I do have a bit of a DULL DAY, I can always just make stuff up. Mr Fullerman calls it

"Using your imagination!"

I'm good at that.

We have *choir* practices to do first, so hopefully no one will mention the HAT again (like Marcus).

I'm going to make a BIG effort to write in my DIARY every day with my non-purple fingers. (For now.)

Just checking... Still OK.

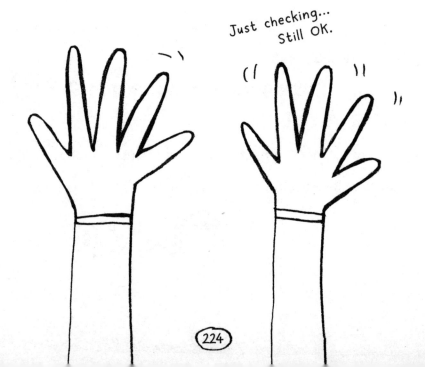

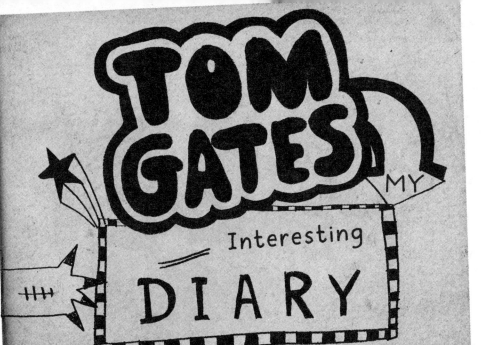

TOM GATES

MY

Interesting

DIARY

Nosey Parkers
NOT WELCOME

All my own
work and life

Dear Diary,

WE WON

THE *choir* COMPETITION!

Can you believe it?

(No.)

We didn't really – I just wanted to write it down and pretend we did, but THAT will never happen.

Mrs Nap has been teaching us some DANCE moves  to go with the song, which has been confusing.

AND the song we're doing is (wait for it...) **"LET'S ALL SING!"** I was shocked and surprised, but it was a popular choice. (No way!)

Mrs Nap said she thought it was a good choice because she'd heard lots of children singing it at break time. Personally, I think "The **BISCUIT** Song" would have been better. We don't sound much like **One Dimension,** though. Some people are finding it tricky just to sing in tune.

La La La

(Marcus.)

At least Mrs Nap has a NEW hat and has stopped asking questions about her old one. PHEW!

Bye for now, Tom

Dear Diary,

Since I've been in the *choir*, I have learnt a
LOT of things – some of them were a bit of a
SURPRISE. ← Surprised face

1. Being in a choir is more **FUN** than I expected.

2. A dress rehearsal doesn't mean you have to
   wear a dress.
   (It was news to Brad Galloway as well.)
   Who knew?

3. Clapping and singing at the same
   time is harder than it looks.

4. Even Marcus Meldrew can't sing out of
   tune **all** the time.

La!

We had our LAST rehearsal today
(missing a bit of our lesson, which was a BONUS
as it was spelling).

It feels like we've practised about
FIVE MILLION TIMES, but
we keep making mistakes. Not as many as the
Recycled Orchestra, though, who are sounding
really ... WONKY. So together we've been
making Mrs Nap and Mr Sprocket look
worried and tired at the end of rehearsals.

Mrs Nap said,   Once more
"Whose idea was it to have a recycled GONG?"

"I think it was yours," Mr Sprocket
told her. The GONG is made from a dustbin
lid that's hung up on a frame, and someone has
to HIT it to make it go BONG!

So far, this hasn't happened at the right time, but when it does work it actually sounds quite GOOD.

We've all been given special T-shirts to wear for the competition.

There's a letter on the front of each one so when we stand in the right order, the T-shirts spell out:

Some T-shirts have STARS ☆ on them, and I've got one of those, so I'm happy about that.

Marcus has an I on his, and he says it stands for (Interesting person.)

I told him it could ALSO stand for (Idiot,) which he didn't think was very funny. (It was a bit funny.)

Mrs Nap told us all to go home and get lots of sleep. "Rest your voices too so you'll be feeling TIPPITY-TOP!"

Derek and I were puzzled because we weren't sure what that meant. Then AMY told us. "She wants us to be at our best."
It makes sense now. (I'll do my best...)
BYE!

Tom

Dear Diary,

 Delia has been **HOGGING** the sofa and TV a lot lately. I TRIED to get her to MOVE ——▸ by colouring my fingers purple 🖊️ with a pen and WAVING them near her face while saying, "LOOK! I've got purple fingers! **PURPLE FINGERS**, purple fingers!"

But she didn't BUDGE at all. It was a mistake to use that pen though, because I can't get it OFF. Washing my hands hasn't worked either.

I've got purple fingers for real now.

Uh-oh.

Looks like I'm STUCK with **purple fingers** for the *choir* competition.

If I wave my hands around a LOT, maybe no one will notice?

 Mum is more excited about the competition than I am. She said,

"I can't wait to hear you all singing."

I'd FORGOTTEN she'd agreed to come along as a helper too.

"Just remember to enjoy yourself, Tom," Mum told me. Then Delia called out from the SOFA, "You might as well because the audience won't!"

Mum told her off for that comment, so it was worth it.   BYE!

From Tom x

Dear Diary,

If my writing is a bit wobbly, it's because I'm writing with a BANDAGE on my finger, which isn't easy. I got my injury during the CHOIR competition while being a bit of a HERO (if I do say so myself). 😊

This is what happened. Read on.

We were supposed to go to the competition on a coach, but it broke down and didn't turn up. Mr Sprocket told us we'd all have to go on the train instead, "Or we'll miss the start of the competition!"

"So let's get M O V I N G!" Mrs Nap said.

"It's ALL going to be FINE.

DON'T PANIC!"

she added, sounding stressed.

Mum was making sure no one got left behind
(like me).

"Come on, slow coach," she kept saying.
But when she started chatting to
Leroy Lewis's mum, I decided it
was a good time to speed up!

"Tom used to sing ALL the time!"

Everyone had to carry the recycled
instruments. The small ones were easy, but the
GONG (dustbin lid) was tricky. It took up a
lot of space on the very crowded train too.

The people going to work were all delighted to see us pile into their carriage.

Mrs Nap decided that now was a good time to do our

 "VOCAL WARM-UPS!"

Oh great.

Which cleared the carriage pretty fast.

La! La la la!

At least we got more space and the people still there got to hear our song.

LET'S ALL SING TOGETHER!

It went down a little better than the warm-ups.

It was an eventful journey. When we left the train, it started to rain, and some of the cardboard instruments got a bit wet.

La! La!

Derek and I volunteered to hold the GONG, which was useful.

We got to the competition hall just as the other schools were arriving. They didn't look DAMP like we did.

"Don't worry, you'll all dry out once you're inside," Mum was telling everyone, hopefully.

Mr Sprocket was keen for us to have a quick practice before the competition started. But that didn't happen. We found our seats and waited to be called up for the rehearsal, but there was a mix-up with another school and we only got ten minutes, and it took FIVE minutes to work out how to get on stage.

But at least we looked good in our T-shirts.

Brad Galloway kept saying,

   "I'm SO NERVOUS, aren't you?"

The more he kept saying it, the more nervous everyone got. Mrs Nap tried to CALM us all down by telling us, "Don't worry, you all know the old saying... A BAD rehearsal means you'll have a GREAT SHOW!"

None of us really understood that, but it sort of calmed some kids down. It wasn't long before the competition began, and we had to wait for our turn to SING. As we sat listening to all the other schools perform, one thing became VERY CLEAR...

OAKFIELD SCHOOL
choir (us) had a very good

chance of coming ▶

LAST.

 "Oh well – what have we got to lose?" I said.

"How BAD can it be?" Derek agreed.

"We'll be OK," AMY told us. "But those schools are really good, aren't they?" she added.

Mrs Nap gave us an inspirational TALK before we went on stage and told everyone to ...

"RELAX!

 Enjoy yourselves and most of all ...

SMILE!"

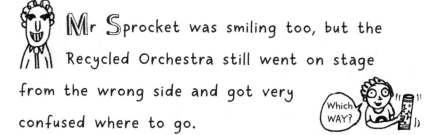

Mr Sprocket was smiling too, but the Recycled Orchestra still went on stage from the wrong side and got very confused where to go.

They took a very long time to get settled and the judges had to wait patiently for the *choir* to walk out as well.

Everyone got completely MUDDLED UP and we all stood in the wrong places, so our T-shirts didn't spell out exactly what they were supposed to.

We spelt out

CROAKFIELD

COOLS

HOHI,

which at least made people laugh.

"**LET'S ALL SING**" didn't go too badly, and we managed to sing the whole song without too many wrong notes and missed dance moves.

The Recycled Orchestra had a few issues with elastic bands _____ SNAPPING

Ping

and some of the boxes and shakers were a bit soggy, and made slightly muffled noises.

Slosh
Slosh

But **Mrs Nap's** HAT was still a super-impressive drum.

When we got to the final note, ♪ someone was supposed to hit the GONG, only they forgot. We kept holding the note for as long as we could, Ahhhh which wasn't easy. Then Marcus decided to hit the GONG himself, only he got carried away... _____

I'll do it!

BONG!

He hit the gong so hard, the head of the hammer flew off like a BALL and was heading straight for me!

I put my hand out to protect myself and ACCIDENTALLY CAUGHT IT WITH ONE HAND.

It was pretty IMPRESSIVE, and I got a BIG ROUND of applause. But my fingers were bashed up by the ball, so Mum took me to get a bandage.

(My fingers weren't that bad, but I enjoyed the attention.)

Everyone thought it was the <u>ball</u> that made my fingers go **PURPLE**. (It was too complicated to explain.) I'll live...

Mr Sprocket and Mrs Nap were very pleased with our PERFORMANCE. "Well done, Oakfield School! You were much better than in rehearsal," Mrs Nap told us, which wasn't saying much.

"It was a VERY HIGH standard. The other schools were really good," he told us. Which is kind of CODE for "don't be disappointed if you come last".

 But amazingly ...

... we were AWARDED a certificate

for the most

CREATIVE PERFORMANCE!

(All down to my expert ball-catch ... maybe.)

Everybody was VERY HAPPY.
Mr Sprocket even did a celebratory
ROBOT dance for us, and we all

CHEERED.

Go, Mr Sprocket!
Go, sir!
Go, sir!

The best part for <u>me</u> was waving my certificate under Delia's nose when we got home.

Choir Certificate

awarded to <u>TOM GATES</u>

FROM OAKFIELD SCHOOL

for the

MOST CREATIVE PERFORMANCE

It was great to share my success with her.

I could tell Delia was very happy for me

even though she didn't show it much.

WAFT
))) WAFT

Look what I WON at the *choir* competition!

Dear Diary,

GOOD NEWS! ☺

My fingers are still slightly **purple**, but my writing is much better. (I will probably never colour my fingers with pen again.)

The Wrinklies have sent us a photo postcard of them doing a double bungee jump on their minibreak. It looks slightly crazy, if you ask me.

Just hanging around...

Wish you were here!

Dad is very impressed that Granddad's wig stayed on.

MORE GOOD NEWS!

THE FOSSILS have actually given us our very

own record player, which is AMAZING!

I'm going to use it at our next

DOGZOMBIES band practice.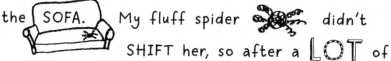

The whole family wants to play their own music

on it. But so far Delia keeps getting

there FIRST and HOGGING up

the SOFA. My fluff spider didn't

SHIFT her, so after a LOT of

thinking, I have finally come up with a very

BIG PLAN that will get Delia back for her

trick AND move her off the sofa to free up the

record player for ME.

(It's a VERY good one. ☺)

I can't wait to see her face.

Love Tom x

Dear Diary,

I AM SO EXCITED

because after such a LONG time of waiting and being very GOOD all the time (and the favourite child), Mum and Dad have finally said

WE CAN GET A

Woof!

DOG!

(YES!)

Not just any kind of dog though – one with lots of lovely **FUR** that I can brush and look after.

I am so happy to get a dog!

To get some practice in, I found a hairbrush in the bathroom and borrowed it to go and BRUSH ROOSTER with. He looked really SMOOTH and well-groomed when I'd finished.

Delia doesn't know anything about the dog yet, but she'll get used to it – eventually. Getting the dog will be the

BEST DAY OF MY LIFE.

Bye for now,

TOM

I casually leave my diary OPEN

somewhere I know Delia will see it.

Then I wait for the ☆ ☺ *FUN* ☆

to begin.

(It doesn't take long.)

I love it when a plan comes together.

(I did use Delia's brush to groom
Rooster, but it was OK - Rooster
didn't catch anything.)

Fluffy fur

How to make a rain stick/shaker

Lid →

① Take an EMPTY crisp tube and make sure the inside is clean. Give it a good wipe and get rid of any crisp crumbs. Take off the lid.

② To decorate your shaker, measure a piece of paper to fit around the outside of the tube.

③ Then colour in the paper and put it to one side.

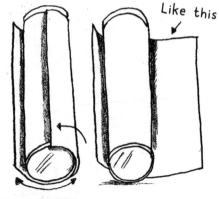

Like this ↙

④ Take the dry rice and a plastic funnel and put the funnel into the top of the tube. Then pour in the rice – don't overfill it or the shaker won't make a good noise.

RICE

⑤ Once it's full, you'll
need to tape the lid back
on very securely with lots
of tape so it doesn't fall off.

Tape

Tape

Don't overfill.
Up to about
here.

⑥ You can use a glue stick to
cover the side of the tube,
then wrap the paper round the
tube and stick
with tape.

Now SHAKE!

TEA CUP TONY AND THE SAUCERS

WATER

Here's a selection of **Teacup Tony's** albums.

Front cover

teacup tony and the saucers
tea cu   ces
Tea   saucers
Tea Cup Tony   he saucers
Tea Cup Ton   the saucers
Tea Cup T   d the saucers
Tea Cup t   nd the saucers
Tea Cup tony   the saucers
Tea Cup Ton   the saucers
tea cup   And the saucers
Tea Cup tony And the saucers.

TEA
CUP
TONY
AND
THE
SAUCERS

Back cover

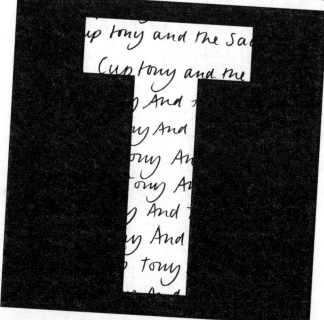

How to play ★BINGO★ or biscuit bingo)

B	I	N	G	O

Empty bingo card.

You can play BINGO with any number of players. One person needs to be the CALLER. Copy the bingo cards to make your own.

Each player has their OWN card. Add the word BINGO and fill in the squares with any numbers between 1 and 50. I've added some biscuits too...

B	I	N	G	O
4	8	29	20	2
50	🍪	9	1	40
3	12	30	7	🍪

B	I	N	G	O

Don't repeat any numbers, though!

NEXT: Write the numbers from 1 to 50 on a piece of paper like in the picture. 1 Then cut them out and fold ↦ 🌀 each number up so you can't see the number.

Do the same for all of them (including the biscuits).

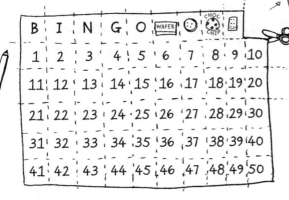

B	I	N	G	O	WAFER	⊙	CHOC CHIP	
1	2	3	4	5	6	7	8	9	10
11	12	13	14	15	16	17	18	19	20
21	22	23	24	25	26	27	28	29	30
31	32	33	34	35	36	37	38	39	40
41	42	43	44	45	46	47	48	49	50

Then place all the numbers in a box.

When all the players have their cards ready, the caller begins by taking one number and calling it out.

The bingo players check their cards and put a cross over any numbers (or biscuits!) they have. The winner is the person who has a <u>full</u> card <u>first.</u>

B	I	N	G	O

BINGO!

NEW book coming out in OCTOBER 2018

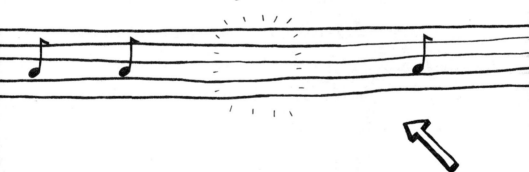

Which ones have <u>YOU</u> read?

Wow! So many.

Bug book shuffle →

All of them!

When Liz was little ⋒, she loved to
draw, paint and make things. Her mum
used to say she was very good at making a mess
(which is still true today!).

She kept drawing and went to art school,
where she earned a degree in graphic design.
She worked as a designer and art director in
the music industry , and her freelance work
has appeared on a wide variety of products.

Liz is the author-illustrator of several
picture books. Tom Gates is the first series of
books she has written and illustrated for older
children. They have won several prestigious
awards ⭐, including the Roald Dahl Funny Prize,
the Waterstones Children's Book Prize, and the
Blue Peter Book Award. The books have been
translated into forty-three languages worldwide.

Visit her at www.LizPichon.com